LAUGHTER AND HAPPY EVER AFTER IN SEABURY

SEABURY - BOOK 9

BETH RAIN

Copyright © 2023 by Beth Rain

Laughter and Happy Ever After in Seabury (Seabury: Book 9)

First Publication: 14th April, 2023

All rights reserved.

No part of this book may be reproduced in any form or by any electronic or mechanical means, including information storage and retrieval systems. Except for use in any review, the reproduction or utilization of this work, in whole or in part, in any form by any electronic, mechanical or other means now known or hereafter invented, is forbidden without the written permission of the publisher.

Published by Beth Rain. The author may be contacted by email on bethrainauthor@gmail.com

❦ Created with Vellum

CHAPTER 1

*L*ou blew out an exhausted breath and dropped the wallpaper scraper she'd been using. As it clattered onto the bare wooden floorboards, the noise - strangely amplified by the empty hallway – made her jump.

'Sorry!' she winced, glancing automatically over her shoulder. 'Idiot!' she added, promptly rolling her eyes at herself.

Who on earth was she apologising to?

There was no one in the cottage but her. Lou lived alone. She had ever since... ever since...

She let out a long, shaky breath. The images rolled in as they always did. Rumpled bed clothes, far too many naked, sweaty limbs, and the twinkle of a nose stud.

'Urgh!'

Lou gave a full-body shudder, trying to shake off

the memory. It had happened well over a year ago, but it still plagued her. Her ex had a lot to answer for! Betrayal for one thing. But, even more serious than catching him in bed with the next-door neighbour's nineteen-year-old daughter, was the fact that he was the reason Lou still felt this constant need to apologise for daring to exist.

It wasn't as though Brendan had ever been particularly awful to her, but towards the end of their almost twenty-year relationship, he'd turned mean. It had been hard to see it at the time, but now that she'd had some space, Lou could see how his undermining, cruel comments had slowly turned her into a husk of who she really was.

No one in Seabury would believe for a single second that Lou had ever become such an apologetic shadow of a person. The minute she'd arrived in town, she'd experienced a mad kind of giddy freedom despite the heartbreak. She'd let her true, bouncy self out to play for the first time in years.

In public, at least.

Here, in the privacy of her own home... well, it was just taking a bit more practise, that was all!

She'd always thought a broken heart would feel more poignant and beautiful in its tragedy – but frankly it just felt like the worst hangover of her life – and it was taking its sweet time to clear the F off.

'I am *not* sorry!' said Lou into the empty space.

Then, for good measure, she blew a loud raspberry, making herself giggle.

Lou had quickly discovered that she *liked* living alone. She *enjoyed* the blissful solitude and the complete lack of disapproving glares and irritated sighs that used to follow her around whenever Brendon was at home.

The problem was, even after all this time, she still had moments where she caught herself being careful not to disturb anybody… or take up too much space… or make too much noise. It was ridiculous. She didn't even *have* any neighbours to annoy with her late-night decorating antics!

The cottage was fairly remote – by Seabury's standards, anyway. Up the hill sat the town allotments, and down the hill was the sea – and that was it, really!

The only house visible from Lou's overgrown back garden was her old rental – and that was going to stay empty for a couple more months at least. She'd rented the place when she'd first come to Seabury, desperate for a refuge while she tried to heal her broken heart. It had been absolutely perfect – almost like living in a gorgeous holiday cottage while she'd thrown herself into her two new jobs. She'd been sad to leave it – but it had always been a short-term deal. Her ex-landlady, Lizzie, had been happy for her to have it while she decided whether to sell the property or move back to town.

The last time Lou had spoken to Lizzie, she had been up to her eyeballs in packing boxes, preparing to return to Seabury after a decade away. So Lou had started hunting for somewhere new – as unlikely as it had seemed at times – she'd managed to find this place. She was now the proud owner of her very own home for the first time in her life.

How grown up?!

Lou pushed her hair away from her hot face, arched her back, and did her best to ease the gnarly knots that seemed to have set up camp along her spine. She prided herself on being relatively fit, but there was something about weeks and weeks of constant, unrelenting DIY that was testing her endurance to the limits. That really was saying something, considering that she voluntarily submitted to the tortures of cold-water swimming with the Chilly Dippers several times a week. On top of that, she took turns with Kate at The Sardine to face the rolling Devon hills on the back of Trixie, the café's delivery tricycle. Even so – it had all been inadequate training for the joys of stripping a bunch of 1970s wallpaper.

Biting her lip, Lou stared at the ragged remains of garish swirls and flowers that still taunted her from the hall walls. Did she have the energy to do any more right now? She really wanted to get this job finished tonight - but by the feel of things, if she didn't have a break, she'd be next to useless in the morning – and that would be a disaster as it was her turn on Trixie.

'Enough!' she yawned, kicking her various tools towards the wall so that she wouldn't manage to stand on them later. She knew she should put them away, but frankly, she didn't have the energy to tidy up after herself only to make the same mess all over again tomorrow.

Letting out another massive yawn, Lou trudged through to the kitchen. It was time to hunt for something to eat and drink - and then maybe a quick bath was in order before she went to bed.

Crossing straight over to the kitchen sink, Lou grabbed a glass from the draining board, filled it to the brim with water and took a gulp. Her kitchen window looked straight out across her back garden towards the sea... or at least, it usually did. She stared in surprise because, right now all she could see was a deep, dark navy blue sky, complete with a few twinkly bits. Night had fallen while she'd been working. Just how late was it?!

Spinning around to peep at the kitsch, custard-yellow clock she'd picked up in the local charity shop, Lou gasped. Ten to midnight?! How was it that late?!

She needed to get to bed... no wonder she was exhausted! Tomorrow would have to be another coffee-fuelled kind of a day.

Just the thought of coffee set Lou's stomach rumbling. When had she last eaten anything? It must have been the bowl of soup and crusty roll she'd had at The Sardine when she'd finished her shift. Blimey... it might be late, but maybe she'd better have something to eat before she went to bed, otherwise she was going to feel all kinds of weird in the morning!

A sandwich maybe? At least that wouldn't take too long. She grabbed a couple of thick slices of crusty bread and, reaching for the jar of chocolate spread, slathered a thick layer on one piece before whacking the other on top.

Grabbing the sandwich, she took an enormous bite, letting out a little groan of delight. Hardly grown up. Hardly healthy. But right now, who cared?! It was nearly midnight and here she was, standing in her own home. That was a pretty amazing feeling – but not something she was going to get used to any time soon.

Lou wondered whether she should head through into her living room and plonk herself on the sofa while she finished her midnight feast. No – maybe not! She had a feeling if she sat down, she'd be asleep in seconds – and she'd regret it in the morning!

Glancing again at the deep blue of the sky outside, she made a snap decision. What could be better than eating a chocolate spread sandwich under the stars?

Unbolting the stable-style kitchen door, Lou pulled it open and stepped out onto the tiny patch of cobbles. It was the only bit of the vast, weed-infested garden she'd managed to tame so far – but it would do the job for tonight.

Staring up at the sprinkling of stars above her, Lou took a deep breath, revelling in the cool, velvety sea air as it gently lifted her hair. She could just about hear the waves shushing at the bottom of the hill – and the sound was like a balm on her nerves, smoothing over the hurt that still lingered there. She still couldn't believe that she got to call this place home. For a moment, she wondered what Brendan would think of her lovely new town and her cosy little cottage with all the jobs that needed doing.

Suddenly, the bread felt like glue in her mouth. Lou struggled to swallow the piece of sandwich as it threatened to get caught in the lump of emotion that had just lodged in her throat.

Damn it! That man wasn't welcome here.

Swallowing hard, Lou cleared her throat, blinked away a couple of tears and took another defiant bite. She stared hard at the dark, shadowy shapes of the garden spread out in front of her. She knew it was there, even if she couldn't see it right now.

She'd been really excited about having so much outdoor space when she'd first stumbled upon Shell Cottage, even if she hadn't quite managed to summon the energy to start clearing it all yet.

The journey to buying this funny little place had been a bit of an odd one – especially considering it was just a stone's throw away from her old rental. Lou had started her property hunt with the local estate agent. He'd dragged her to all the surrounding areas – stating that her budget was nowhere near enough to buy somewhere in Seabury itself. They'd trudged around grotty flats in nearby towns, investigated tiny terraces, and even been to have a look at a hideous new build that had instantly brought Lou out in a rash of pure loathing.

One afternoon – just as she was about to give up and start hunting for somewhere to rent instead – Lou had gone out for a stomp in the hills above Seabury. She'd wandered the slopes, hoping the wintry fields and crashing sea below would calm her fears about having to leave the little town she'd fallen in love with.

As though some kind of magic was at work that day, her steps had led her in a giant circle, all the way back to this cottage. It was tucked away below the allotments and sat at the end of a rutted lane that no one seemed to have been down for several years.

Lou had peered over the stone walls across the jungle of a garden, at the tiny cottage beyond. It had looked abandoned... and like a lot of work...

Just six weeks later – she had the keys in her hands.

According to her estate agent, it was a "unique opportunity" and "charmingly rustic". When she'd asked the locals, though, they'd told her it had been empty for years – a part of someone's estate that the relatives had precisely zero interest in. It was vastly overpriced and had been on the market for so long that the estate agent had forgotten it was even on their books.

Fuelled by a dream of owning her own patch of Seabury and living in a cottage overlooking the sea, Lou made an offer for the place – well under the asking price but still right at the top end of her budget. Much to everyone's surprise, it had been accepted a week later.

And so, Lou's relationship with scrapers and filler and paint rollers had begun. She loved her little house... but that wasn't to say that she didn't get waves of pure overwhelm when she thought about all the work she still needed to do on it.

It really was absolutely tiny. The kitchen was little more than a lean-to that looked as though it had been added to the side of the cottage as an afterthought. She'd managed to squeeze her two-seater sofa into the living room right in front of the open fireplace – but there was little room for anything else. The hallway with its horrible wallpaper had just enough space to get the front door open without tripping over the foot of the stairs that led up to the second floor.

Lou liked the stairs. They were narrow and wooden, and swept up and around a tight corner directly into her bedroom where it was tucked up under the eaves. Just past her bed, a wooden door led through to the bathroom, which boasted a rose-pink vintage bath, basin and loo – which Lou secretly adored even though it had horrified the estate agent when he'd spotted it.

The main problem with the place being quite so small was that there simply wasn't room for all her stuff. Luckily, there was an old, attached garage on the side of the house. Sure, there was a hole in the roof over to one side, but she'd managed to pile a lot of her boxes on the other side and covered everything with a tarpaulin – just in case.

There were benefits to it being quite so cosy, of course. Every single bit of DIY she completed got the place closer to feeling like home. The cottage was quickly becoming her refuge - somewhere she was happy to come back to at the end of her very busy days. With her two jobs – at The Sardine and The Pebble Street Hotel – Lou had many late nights and early starts, but it was always nice to turn the key in the front door of Shell Cottage and shrug out of her coat.

If only she had a tiny bit more room, then it really would be perfect. Maybe tidying up the garden would help with that. It wasn't as though she had any grand plans for it – after all, she didn't have any gardening experience. The house she'd shared with Brendan didn't have much of a garden… well, it did, but the treacherous idiot had paved over it because he didn't like having to push a lawnmower around.

Lou had tried to brighten the space up with some potted plants, but they never lasted long – the slugs seemed to be quite fond of them. She couldn't really blame them, considering there was absolutely nothing else left for them to eat.

She hadn't seen any slugs out here, though. That said, it was so overgrown there could be a slug the size of a Shetland pony just meters away and she would be none the wiser.

As usual, thoughts of her old home and her ex-boyfriend made Lou feel like she'd just got a puncture somewhere in her soul. No matter how much work she did on this place - how many little victories she had over the old plumbing – memories of Brendan still managed to make her feel completely worthless.

Lou let out a long sigh. She was just tired. That's all it was. She needed to go to bed. She'd figure out what to do about the garden another time… maybe in the morning over breakfast… if she woke up early enough to have any!

Turning her back on the magical sight of the navy-blue sky and stars stretching into infinity over the invisible but ever-present sea, Lou dragged her feet back inside the cottage. Doing her best to ignore the half-stripped hallway, she finally climbed the steep stairs and fell into bed.

CHAPTER 2

'Morning sleepyhead!' laughed Kate as Lou stumbled into The Sardine, yawning her head off.

'Sorry!' she gasped. 'Blimey – that one was like being body snatched!'

Kate chuckled and without asking turned to the Italian Stallion – the café's vintage coffee machine. She quickly set it whirring and whistling.

'Cappuccino with extra chocolate sprinkles on its way!' said Kate over the noise. 'Give me just two seconds and emergency caffeine will be deployed!'

Lou grinned at Kate and took a deep, cake-and-coffee-scented breath as she looked around the little café. She adored The Sardine – the time she spent here never felt like work. She'd bounced in here on her second day in Seabury, high on a strange mixture of pure joy and absolute grief, and had somehow managed to secure herself a job. In fact, Kate had practically pounced on her.

Lou had become a part of The Sardine family – working alongside Kate, Sarah and Ethel as they served their regulars in the minuscule café, delivered sandwiches all over the district on Trixie the tricycle, and built up Kate's brand-new venture – The Sardine's Cake Subscription box. Lou had enjoyed every second of it.

'You still up for doing the rounds today?' asked Kate, popping the drink down on the table in front of her and eyeing Lou in concern. 'You look a bit done in. I don't mind doing it if you need a bit of an easier morning in here?'

Lou grinned at her friend and shook her head. 'I'm absolutely fine!' she said. 'Nothing a good coffee and a ride on Trixie won't fix, anyway.'

'Are you not sleeping well?' said Kate, clearly determined to make sure she was okay.

'Like a log – don't worry about that,' said Lou truthfully. 'When I remember to actually go to bed, that is! I got home from my shift at Pebble Street last night and decided to attack the hallway - I lost track of time. It was midnight before I realised that I hadn't even had any tea, let alone done anything else!'

'Ah!' laughed Kate. 'Been there, done that!'

'Yeah, I bet!' chuckled Lou.

Kate and her boyfriend Mike had recently moved to the old lighthouse that overlooked Seabury. It had been

Kate's childhood dream to live there – a dream Mike had brought to life for her. But that didn't mean there wasn't an awful lot of work to do to turn the old industrial building into a family home for the couple and Mike's teenage daughter, Sarah.

In fact, Lou and Kate had bonded even further over DIY how-to tips since she'd bought the cottage, and Kate had lent her all manner of tools she needed to complete the tasks as they had come up.

'You know,' said Kate, 'you could always get Ben to finish off some of the DIY bits you don't have time for?'

'Never!' gasped Lou in mock outrage, shaking her head. She adored Ben – and as he was both the town's favoured handyman as well as the other half of Hattie over at Pebble Street – it would make sense on paper. But Lou felt like she had something to prove when it came to her little cottage. 'I know it's taking me ages, but I'm loving the fact that it's all down to me. I feel like I'm getting to know my little home and all its quirks. At least by the time I'm done, I'll have had hand in making the place completely mine – and I'll know it inside and out.'

Kate nodded. 'I get it – and I admire your energy… just…' she paused.

'What, boss?' chuckled Lou. She knew there was something Kate wasn't saying.

'Just… don't burn yourself out, will you!' she said, raising her eyebrows. 'Two jobs, riding Trixie, swimming with the Dippers and everything else you do. I mean – shout if you need a hand with anything – we're all here to help, you know.'

'I know, but...' Lou started awkwardly.

'No buts,' said Kate.

'Okay. No buts,' said Lou gratefully.

She might have lived in Seabury for more than a year now, but the community here still took her breath away – especially the way it seemed to have claimed her as one of its own.

Taking a huge sip of coffee, Lou sighed with relief. 'Actually – I was thinking this morning that I might have to ask someone for a bit of advice on the garden. I can handle doing the internal DIY... but I think I've got to admit that mess is beyond me!'

'Good idea!' said Kate, starting to line up the sandwich orders on the counter, ready to stash them in Trixie's trailer for the delivery round. 'Have you got any plans for it?'

'There are these lovely shrubs... you know... the ones with the red flowers?' she said vaguely.

'You really weren't joking when you said you don't know anything about gardens, were you?!' said Kate, starting to giggle.

Lou shrugged good-naturedly and shook her head. 'Not a clue. And I've got no idea what they're called, but I'm determined to find out. I always wanted them and my ex... well, for one thing, he preferred paving slabs to living things. Said they made too much of a mess.'

Kate blew out an angry noise, and Lou decided to change the subject. Her friend knew the story of what had driven her here to Seabury, but Lou had always glossed over the whole thing with a thick layer of bravado. She didn't want people's pity – so she always did her best to turn the betrayal that had left an ugly bruise on her heart into a joke whenever she was forced to tell the story. Still – she was so tired today, she didn't have the energy for the coverup.

'I think I'd like to make the lawn a bit bigger too… I think there used to be a small patch, though it's waste-high at the moment… after that, I've got no idea what's under there. It'd be lovely to flatten it out a bit and buy some garden furniture… maybe one of those big umbrella things and some chairs to lounge around in…'

Kate was nodding, but even as Lou tested the idea out loud, she could feel herself wrinkling her nose up. She hated sitting around in the sun. It wasn't her thing at all.

'You don't look convinced!' said Kate.

'I'm not. I prefer curling up somewhere cosy if I can… though a bit of indoor-outdoor space would be nice… the cottage is so small.'

Lou sighed. She was starting to feel overwhelmed again. She had all these ideas, but until she knew what was hiding in the undergrowth beyond her back door, there was no way she could make any decisions about what she actually wanted.

'I've got all these ideas...' she sighed

'You say that like it's a bad thing!' said Kate, starting to stack fresh scones on the cake stand on the counter.

'It is – if I can't ever make up my mind,' Lou laughed.

'Just enjoy the fact that you can do whatever you want. It's all yours – and there's no one to tell you what you can or can't do with the place,' said Kate.

'It's totally up to me...' said Lou. She knew it, of course, but hearing Kate say it out loud was exciting. 'I get to do whatever I want.'

'Yup!' said Kate. 'Whenever you want, too. Totally at your own speed... which, as far as I can tell... is at the speed of light.'

Lou snorted. Her friend might not have known her for long in the grand scheme of things, but Kate certainly had a good handle on what she was like.

Lou wasn't a dawdler. She liked to go at life hell-for-leather. If she decided to try something, that was it – she went all in. Brendan had hated that about her... which was probably why she'd packed every single day here in Seabury with as much fun and adventure as she could manage to squeeze in.

'You know... I was thinking...' said Lou.

'Uh oh – that sounds dangerous!' said Kate, raising her eyebrows.

'It's just... well, the allotments are just up the hill from the cottage – and I know quite a few of them through the hotel... I mean, they're always turning up and dropping off fresh goodies for Hattie to cook with.' Lou paused and scratched her nose. She was so bad at asking for help – even if it was just testing the waters with a friend.

'Spit it out, Lou!' chuckled Kate.

'Well… do you reckon someone up there might be able to help me with the garden? Just to get things started, I mean?' she said.

'Of course!' said Kate with a shrug. 'You know what they're like – they live for their allotments and planting and all that… though… you might want to make sure you ask the right person. I mean, there are people up there who're die-hard into one thing. I heard one of them just grows broad beans… and I'm guessing that isn't one of the many *many* ideas you've had for your back garden!'

Lou pulled a face and shook her head.

'Why don't you ask Charlie?' said Kate. 'He knows all of them up there… he's bound to steer you to the right person.'

'You don't think he'd mind?' said Lou.

'Mind?' laughed Kate. 'You have *met* Charlie, right? If anything he'd be gutted if you didn't ask him.'

'Okay,' said Lou, with a nod. 'Okay – maybe I will next time I see him.'

'Well… why don't you swing past the allotments when you've done the delivery round?' said Kate. 'He's got a box of veggies for me for tomorrow's soup for the Dippers anyway. I think he was planning on bringing it down this afternoon, but if you're out and about and you don't mind...?'

'Mind?!' said Lou. 'Thank you, that'd be absolutely brilliant. Plus – you know I like my soup after a swim!'

'Need more coffee before you head out?' asked Kate, as she did a quick final check of all the orders before packing them into two large baskets ready to be placed into Trixie's trailer.

'I'm good,' said Lou, shaking her head. Kate's plan along with the super-strong caffeine hit had given her some much-needed bounce back. She stepped forward and grabbed the baskets from the counter.

'Right – you head off and I'll start breakfast for the lovebirds,' said Kate, shooting a smile towards the café door.

'Eh?' said Lou, turning slowly so that she didn't knock anything over in the cramped space. 'Oh! Morning Lionel! Mary!'

'After you!' Lionel called to her, holding the door wide open so that she could sidle out sideways.

'You're a gent – thanks Lionel,' said Lou, shooting them both a smile.

Mary beamed back at her as she wrapped her fingers around Lionel's arm. Lou felt something in her heart give a twinge. If ever there was a couple who could make her believe in true love again, it was these two. The peppery ex-headmistress had softened so much since the pair of them had finally mended the relationship that had started decades ago.

'You two have a wonderful day,' she said, beaming at them.

'Always!' said Lionel, without taking his eyes off Mary.

Lou almost swooned on the spot. 'Right... must dash,' she said. 'I've gotta see a man about a garden...'

'Off to see our Charlie, eh?' said Lionel.

Lou grinned. Okay – so it was official – he was *definitely* the man to ask.

∼

Lou arrived at the allotments a couple of hours later. She was panting, but her delivery baskets were completely empty apart from the paper bag full of goodies Kate had insisted on adding in as a surprise for Charlie.

Lou pulled through the gateway and left Trixie next to the hedge, giving the tricycle's handlebars a fond pat as she went. She made her way along the neatly edged, grassy path towards Charlie's patch. Sure enough, she spotted him immediately, bent double as he secured a spindly looking something or other to a short bamboo cane with some twine.

'Hello Lou!' he called with a smile so broad that it made the wrinkles fan around his eyes. 'What brings you up here? I've not forgotten anything for The Sardine have I? Or the hotel...? I can never keep up with where you're working from one minute to the next!'

'Nothing like that,' said Lou, grinning at him. 'I'm just on my way back from the delivery rounds for Kate... and she suggested I popped in for her box of ingredients as I wanted to pick your brain about something anyway.'

'Oh!' said Charlie. 'Wonderful. I'll just get them from the shed. Two secs.'

He dashed off before Lou could say anything else, so she clutched the paper bag of goodies, feeling like a bit of a lemon as she stared across the well-tended plots. They were all so different. Some had plants lined up like rows of soldiers, and others looked far less formal, with flowers and veggies all dotted in, seemingly at random.

Charlie's was gorgeous. She thought it looked like something you might find outside of a Hobbit hole – all cosy, cottage garden vibes, with bright flowers trailing from the window boxes of his shed, while lines of pea-sticks gave it an old-fashioned sense of order. It certainly beat the plot just down the hill... which looked like it had been covered in 1970s swirly carpet for some reason. No... she had to be wrong... she clearly didn't know what she was talking about!

'Right!' said Charlie, reappearing from the shed and triumphantly waving a packed cardboard box at her. 'This little lot should make you bunch of daft beggars a soup to warm the cockles of your heart tomorrow morning!'

'Charlie – you're a marvel!' said Lou, staring down into the box of goodies – some fresh and some from his precious stores.

'Ah – get away with you!' he laughed.

'Not before I've handed you these,' said Lou, passing over the bag of cakes Kate had sent.

Charlie took it, peeped inside and smiled.

'All my favourites,' he said in delight. 'Thank you – my packed lunch from Ethel has just got a whole lot better! Just don't tell her I said that!' he added quickly.

Lou grinned at him. She knew he was joking – Ethel always sent him off with gorgeous sandwiches and at least two slices of fresh, homemade cake.

'And…' said Lou, suddenly feeling nervous for some strange reason, 'I was wondering if I could ask for your advice on something? Well… your help, really…'

'Of course!' said Charlie, looking even more delighted than he had when he'd spotted the bagful of cakes.

'Well, it's about the garden at Shell Cottage,' she said. 'It's a bit beyond me if I'm honest. I was wondering if there might be someone up here who'd be willing to help me out a bit? With you being the chair of the allotment association… I thought you might be able to steer me in the right direction?'

'You've come to the right person,' said Charlie,

frowning slightly as he absentmindedly scratched the white bristles on his chin. Clearly, this was a much more complicated question than Lou had anticipated. 'This wants some thinking about,' he said, thrusting his hand into the paper bag and pulling out one of Sarah's triple-chocolate fudge brownies before offering the bag to her.

Lou shook her head, but when Charlie rattled the bag at her encouragingly, she dipped her hand in and chose a piece of Ethel's orange shortbread.

'Good choice!' said Charlie, nodding his appreciation. 'Now then – this all rather depends on what you want to get out of the garden, to be honest,' he said, taking a bite and munching away. 'If you wanted to grow broad beans-'

'I really don't!' said Lou quickly.

'Well then – that rules out Jean!' he said. 'And I'd say there's not much point asking Ben. Poor lad – he'd want to help you and would move heaven and earth, but he's got even more jobs than you have – and that boat of his…'

'And Hattie!' chuckled Lou. Hattie was both her best friend and boss at The Pebble Street Hotel – Head Chef extraordinaire – as well as Ben's other half.

'Exactly. The poor lad barely has time to breathe as it is.'

Lou nodded. It was partly why she hadn't already asked him. Ben had the kind of knack where he could turn his hand to everything – which made him possibly the most popular handyman to have ever lived.

'And you don't want to ask Cyril Nolan either,' he said. 'Unless you want to cover everything in carpet and leave it all to die off for a few years!'

'So that *is* carpet!' said Lou, pointing at the swirling paisley a little way down the hill.

'Afraid so,' sighed Charlie. 'Not the way I'd go about it, but it's his answer to everything. He used to be a carpet salesman and his son's still in the business… so he gets a good rate!'

Lou snorted and Charlie winked at her as he popped the last bit of brownie in his mouth and chewed thoughtfully.

'I know – I think you'd be best asking Sean White – he's on the Paths and Sheds subcommittee up here – and he was a professional gardener at one point too,' said Charlie. 'He'd be a good place to start. Even if he can't help you himself, he might be able to point you in the right direction.'

Lou nodded, frowning slightly. 'You know that name rings a bell,' she said, staring across the different plots in the direction of her little cottage. She couldn't quite see it from all the way up here – but she knew it was tucked away in the fold of the hill as it led down towards the sea.

'Sean's like you,' said Charlie, raising a bemused eyebrow. 'Loves himself a dip in the sea – and doesn't seem to care that it's cold enough to shrink his gooseberries to the size of redcurrants.'

Lou let out a splutter of surprised laughter. She was

going to have to save that one to share with the Dippers the next morning.

'Of course!' she said at last, fighting the giggles. 'That's where I've heard his name before. He's often out swimming when we are!'

'That's more than likely,' said Charlie. 'And he takes it seriously!'

Lou nodded. That was true. Sean swam on his own and tended to keep himself to himself. And boy – did he swim. Most of the Dippers – including her - plodded into the water with screams and squeals and splashed about before high-tailing it back to The Sardine for a steaming bowl of soup, or a coffee and cake calorie fix. Not Sean though – he swam for ages – and he only rocked up in The Sardine when Stanley, Kate's big, fluffy Bernese Mountain Dog, joined him for a swim.

'Stanley!' said Lou, nodding vaguely.

'You've lost me,' said Charlie with a frown.

'Sean's brought Stanley back to Kate in the café a couple of times when he's met him out swimming! That's where I've seen him before! I mean… I've not met him – but I've seen him from a distance a few times and caught a glimpse of him bundling Stanley back through the door of the café!'

She went quiet. Yes – she'd definitely spotted him… perfect bum, strong body…

'More than likely!' said Charlie, interrupting her thoughts. 'That dog thinks he's a mermaid! Sean told me Stanley's often down there on the beach waiting for him to arrive for his swim! Anyway – I'd say he's your man to help with the garden – or at least point you in the right direction. He's not up here at the moment or I'd introduce the pair of you.'

'That's okay,' said Lou, hefting the box of veggies up onto her hip. 'I'm bound to run into him sooner or later – this is Seabury after all!'

CHAPTER 3

Lou chucked her swimming cap with the ridiculous plastic flowers into her bag along with her huge striped beach towel and made a dash for her front door. She adored her early-morning sea swims with the Chilly Dippers and didn't want to be late.

After her long cycle on Trixie the day before, she'd decided to treat herself to an evening off any DIY, and as it was her night off from Pebble Street too, Lou had fallen into bed early.

Still... she couldn't exactly claim to have had a good sleep. For some reason, Sean White's face had swum in front of her eyes. Okay, okay... maybe not just his face!

The man was fit. But then, that wasn't really surprising with the amount of swimming he did, was it?! Charlie had been right when he'd said Sean was serious about it.

Lou was pretty much at the opposite end of the spectrum - she tended to run into the sea and prance about in the shallows like an idiot for quite a while before one of the others managed to coax her in for a decent dip. Even so, she'd always be wrapped in her massive towel and stuffing her face with the most calorie-laden treat she could get her hands on before Sean even thought about emerging from the sea. One thing was for sure – he certainly didn't have a spare inch of flesh on him. He was all taut and firm. Even from a distance, it hadn't escaped her notice.

The pair of them hadn't met, even though she'd spotted him wandering past her house a few times – clearly taking an alternative route up to the allotments. Other than these brief sightings, she knew next to nothing about him.

Well... she did now! She knew that he was on the Paths and Sheds committee. Dull or what?! Talk about an anti-climax – in more ways than one! That reality certainly didn't match up with the rather distracting dreams she'd been having about him last night. Somehow, being on that committee made it sound like he'd have one of those high-pitched, nasal voices. Hell - he probably even had a train set laid out in his attic.

Lou shuddered as she pulled her front door closed behind her with a *thunk* and began to route march her way down her little lane. The idea of getting someone like *that* to help her out at the cottage felt a bit too much like inviting the ghost of her ex in again. A weaselly little good-for-nothing idiot...

Lou shook her head, suddenly cross with herself. Just because Brendan had turned out to be a total twonk didn't mean every guy was the same... even if they were on the Paths and Sheds committee!

Still... it was a shame Sean sounded like a bit of a berk... because he certainly looked nice in a pair of swimming shorts. Even on a blustery October day in the piddling rain, he'd cut a remarkably fine figure running down the beach and diving into the waves. Sure – he didn't look so good with his swimming goggles on - but frankly, no one in the known universe could manage to look good in a pair of those!

Lou rather liked his hair too. It was thick and dark and a little bit curly. It always stood on end when he towelled it dry... Weird. She'd obviously noticed a lot more about Sean than she realised!

Not that it really mattered of course. Lou was a strictly no-man kinda girl these days. She'd had enough of all that nonsense with Brendan – she'd wasted years of her life fitting into someone else's plan and doing her best to make herself smaller to make him happy. It was like she'd had to dull her shine just so that he didn't look quite so crap in comparison. Well – no more! Lou was going to be the loud and proud sparkly unicorn she'd always wanted to be – and sod anyone who didn't like it!

Unfortunately, swimming mornings weren't the

best for feeling all glamorous and empowered. What was the point when she'd be stripping down to her swimsuit and getting wet and sandy? And, of course, mascara was a definite no-no unless she wanted to resemble a half-drowned panda for the rest of the day!

Lou pulled the ginormous brown cardigan she was wearing tightly around herself. It was probably the ugliest piece of clothing she owned and she knew that it made her look a bit like someone's great aunty Mildred – but it was super-warm and the morning air was chilly. Instead of the fresh, blue-sky day she'd been hoping for, the clouds were leaden and the breeze wasn't so much a gentle tickle as an insistent poke in the ribs.

Speeding up, Lou's wellies flapped around her calves. The Dippers were planning to swim from North Beach today – so the wellies were a must. North Beach was covered in large pebbles. It was an absolute nightmare to navigate your way down to the sea without sustaining a stubbed toe or two. Lou had learned early on that the simplest solution was to wear a pair of old wellies right down to the water's edge and kick them off right at the last moment. They were probably the grossest things she owned considering they constantly had a pair of damp, salty, sandy feet in them – but as far as Lou was concerned, they were a lifeline.

As she made her way down the hill and hurried along the front of West Beach, Lou cast the sandy stretch a longing look. She much preferred it when they swam at this end of town. The sand was gentle and you could wade for ages before having to commit to actually swimming. But the one or two slightly more serious swimmers far preferred North Beach. Yes, the pebbles were a pain – but they disappeared pretty fast when you got into the water – and you were up past your knicker line before you knew it!

'You made it!' called Doris from the Post Office the moment Lou clambered down the steps and began to trudge across the pebbles towards the gaggle of women who were gathered around the wooden hulk of an abandoned boat. The old thing had been slowly disintegrating on the beach ever since the first day Lou had arrived in town.

She grinned at the sight. The sky above may be the same colour as the pebbles, but this intrepid lot had all stripped down to their costumes. Some of them had their swim caps in place, while others were still sporting bobble hats. There was a decent amount of raised arm hair and goosebumps on show – today definitely wasn't one to hang around gossiping!

'Not so sure about this today,' said Lou lightly to Doris, as she reluctantly shed her big brown cardigan and top layers, then dropped her jeans to reveal her ancient and slightly saggy swimming costume underneath. She'd had it for far too long – it was well past time for an upgrade – and yet, there didn't seem to be much point.

'Ooh,' said one of the other women, pointing a little way along the beach. 'Look – Adonis is back again!'

Lou peered over while simultaneously trying to pull her wellies back onto her bare feet – almost face-planting into the pebbles in the process. It seemed Seabury was working its magic again. She needed to speak to Sean – and there he was – in his full, swim-suited glory!

Straightened up, Lou raised her hand and waved at him.

'Do you *know* Sean?!' said Doris in surprise.

'Oh,' said Lou, dropping her hand. 'No – I don't... but...'

Why had she just waved like a lunatic?!

This was not the best time to introduce herself, was it? She hardly looked her best – standing here wearing her saggy cossie and wellies, gently turning blue while certain parts of her anatomy registered their protest at being quite so cold.

Damnit!

Sean was waving back... rather uncertainly, it had to be said... but now she was going to have to go and talk to him, wasn't she? Lou pulled her towel around herself in the vague hope that it might hide the pointy bits.

'Are we ready?' she said to the chattering group, deciding to ignore the man now watching her with a decidedly puzzled look on his face.

'Blimey, girl!' said one of them. 'Bit keen, ain't you?'

Lou grinned and, with a shrug, began to amble towards the line where the water was bashing grumpily against the pebbles. She wasn't even sure if Sean was still looking her way, but when she unwound her towel, she definitely did it with a bit more flare than usual… just in case. Dropping it to the pebbles, she chanced a glance in his direction – only to see him striding purposefully for the waves. How on earth was he doing that without breaking his feet in the process?!

Lou watched as Sean waded straight in up to his knees without so much as a shudder. She was impressed. Member of the Paths and Sheds committee or not, he had some balls on him… or at least, he would until the cold water got to work on shrinking them into nothingness!

Sean paused for a moment, staring intently ahead of him. As soon as the next wave bashed around him, in he dove – straight under the water.

Lou let out an involuntary squeak. There was *no way* she could ever do that. She liked to make the adjustment a lot more gently. Ankles first – then knees. Then she'd inch forwards until she had no choice but to dip down and squeal as the salty water reached over the knicker line of her costume. That was the bit she hated the most. After that, it was usually plain sailing for about five minutes – until it was time to hot foot it back to her towel and a nice bowl of soup in The Sardine.

Sean reappeared above the water.

'Oops!' she muttered as he turned to look in her direction as though could sense her eyes on him. She quickly looked away. Damn it! Now she had no choice – she didn't want him to think she was a wuss after seeing him dive straight in like that – she wanted to look brave and fearless.

Without thinking about it too much, Lou waded straight into the freezing water and, taking a deep breath, she followed his example and dove straight in.

Seconds later, she resurfaced gasping for breath, willing her heart to keep beating. It was so cold, everything felt like it had stopped working. She could barely breathe – but she could hear the hoots and cheers of the other Chilly Dippers, all applauding her bravery.

'Get in there, my girl!' cheered Doris. 'You're a natural!'

'What on earth's got under your skin this morning?' laughed an elderly woman called Sally, as she dabbled around in the shallows, her long grey plats pinned to the top of her head with a giant crocodile clip.

'You've turned into a dolphin since last week!' shouted another.

Lou would have loved to acknowledge their kind comments... but right at that moment, she didn't have any air in her lungs. Gasping, she peeped in Sean's direction, but he was already swimming steadily for the far end of North Beach, so she had no idea if he'd even seen her heroics in action.

Still – this did seem like the perfect opportunity to talk to him. She could swim over there, introduce herself and see if he'd give her a hand with her garden. It killed two birds with one stone after all – because she really needed to get moving if she wasn't going to freeze to death!

Lou hated getting her hair wet when she was swimming – that's why she had her swimming cap – and she didn't like putting her face in the water either. Together, these two things meant that anything other than an ungainly breaststroke was practically impossible. She'd just have to go as fast as her crampy legs would kick.

Setting off in Sean's direction, Lou began pulling herself through the swell with as much strength as she could muster. The waves kept pushing her back towards the shore, and she wasn't strong enough to fight them, so it wasn't long before she was doing a strange kind of swim-run as her feet found the bottom. She did her best to propel herself along, trying to ignore the fact that she probably looked like a total idiot. There was no way she was giving up now, though!

Just as she was nearly close enough to call Sean's name, he disappeared under the surface of the water. Lou kept swimming steadily towards the spot where he'd gone under… but… nothing. Seconds drifted by and she started to tread water, staring around her, wondering when on earth he was going to come up for air. Then the seconds started to feel more like minutes... and there weren't any bubbles.

Shit!

Maybe he'd been attacked by a shark or something. No – she was being an idiot – there weren't any sharks around Seabury. But... there was always a first time for everything, wasn't there? Or maybe he had cramp and needed saving.

Gah – this was awful!

Lou looked all around her, her arms and legs starting to ache from treading water for so long. Nope – there wasn't a sign of him anywhere. She had to do something – but what?!

Then she remembered that awful show Brendan used to watch – full of fit young women in tight swimsuits, dashing around rescuing people. Lou had never paid much attention, but right now she was doing her best to remember what they did after all the running around. She needed to dive. She needed to find Sean and get him to the surface.

Taking a deep breath, Lou did an awkward dive forwards, doing her best to keep her eyes open as she did so.

Thud!

She came up with a spluttering squeal of pain – only to come face to face with a decidedly flustered Sean with his goggles half off where she'd smashed straight into him.

Lou splashed around, trying to keep her head above

the waves while she coughed up mouthfuls of salty water. She did her best not to knock into Sean again as she spluttered. He remained a bit too close for comfort, rubbing the bridge of his nose and staring at her with a mixture of confusion and concern.

'You okay?'

Lou nodded, trying to catch her breath as the next wave picked her up and practically dumped her on top of him. Again, there was a confused jumble of skin and limbs as they did their best not to go under. Lou started to cough again.

'Sorry,' said Lou, breathing heavily. 'I thought you were drowning...!'

Sean was too busy trying not to laugh while checking she was okay to say anything. Then Lou let out a squeal as something brushed behind her, and she clung to Sean in case it really was a shark.

It wasn't – it was Stanley. He was paddling around them in circles and seemed determined to wedge himself under her arm somehow.

'I think he's trying to rescue you!' laughed Sean.

'Silly fluff!' coughed Lou. 'I'm fine, I'm fine!'

'Come on – let's get back to the beach,' said Sean. 'Before Stanley starts trying to tow you out!'

CHAPTER 4

'You know, you could have just said "hello!"' said Sean, as he placed a large bowl of soup down on the table in front of her.

Lou smiled at him in pure embarrassment. She picked up her spoon and slurped down a mouthful of scalding hot soup as she watched him return to the counter for his coffee.

The pair of them had decided to retreat to The Sardine after their underwater head-on collision. A soaking-wet Stanley had glued himself to her side all the way back and had kept casting uneasy looks at her as if he was waiting for her to collapse in a heap every time she coughed.

Now, the big soggy dog was curled up for a post-rescue snooze – his giant, wet, furry body draped across her feet. It was quite sweet really.

Lou had managed to dry off a bit and had yanked

off her awful swim cap at the earliest opportunity – though she almost wished she'd just left it on. Heavens only knew what state her hair was in – probably all sticking up at the sides and flat on top. How was that fair, given that Sean looked practically edible post-swim? The only tell-tale marks left on him were a couple of angry red rings around his eyes where she'd managed to ram his goggles into his face when she'd crashed into him.

With a quick check that Sean was still busy chatting to Kate – Lou leaned back in her chair, balancing it on two legs as she did her best to investigate the state of her reflection in the café window. It was practically impossible, given the fact that her feet were pinned to the floor by a snoozing canine, but from the unwelcome flash she did manage to catch of herself – things looked like they might be even worse than she'd feared.

Lou quickly righted herself and did her best to flatten her hair with her hands. Maybe if she pressed hard enough, she might be able to iron it back into place. She didn't really know why she was bothering. No matter how bad she looked – she couldn't really top the fact that she'd nearly drowned the person she'd been trying to save... the person who'd just reappeared at her table and was busy grinning at her.

Lou returned the smile, wishing that for once she could just do things in the normal way. Couldn't she have just waited until she was fully dressed... and maybe wearing a little bit of mascara? Oh no – she had to make a complete tit out of herself, didn't she?!

'I'm so sorry I ruined your swim,' she said, suddenly feeling a bit shy of this fit, cute man who'd had to hold her up while she'd been wearing her saggy swimsuit and hat with plastic flowers all over it.

'There's always tomorrow – the sea isn't going anywhere,' Sean shrugged.

Lou smiled at him. He did have a point – though she'd never thought about it quite like that before. She wasn't sure what else to say, so she took another spoonful of the hot soup to keep her mouth busy, shooting sly little looks at him as he sipped his coffee.

She had to admit – so far so gorgeous! There wasn't any sign of the squeaky, nasal voice she'd feared, and he hadn't mentioned a secret love of model railways yet either. In fact – Sean seemed to be fairly normal... but not in a bad way.

'Charlie mentioned you might want to talk to me about your garden?' said Sean, after the silence had gone on a bit too long to be comfortable.

Lou smiled. That hadn't taken long! She should have known that he would have already been given the heads-up – this was Seabury after all, and it had been more than twelve hours since she'd mentioned it to Charlie. She opened her mouth to start explaining, but right at that moment the door of the little café flew open and the rest of the Chilly Dippers piled in.

'Skiver!' said Doris accusingly as she stared from

Lou's half-eaten bowl of soup to Sean and then to her. 'Oh... *I* see where your priorities lie!'

Lou could feel her cheeks starting to flame, but Sean just grinned at the newcomers. 'Coffees are on me this morning!' he said, garnering a general round of cheers from the slightly blue, shivering newcomers.

Lou looked at Sean as he started to field the round of grateful and cheeky comments with ease.

'You know – you can't just buy us with a coffee!' chuckled Doris. 'Not when you're busy poaching our members.'

'Oh yes he can!' shouted someone from over by the door. 'You're welcome to Lou every week if we get free cakes in exchange for her!'

'Charming!' chuckled Lou.

As the Chilly Dippers flooded Kate and Sarah with their various orders, Lou turned her attention back to Sean and did her best to ignore the curious glances that kept being thrown their way.

'Sorry,' she said, shooting a shy smile at him, 'what were we talking about?'

'Your garden!' laughed Sean. 'Charlie mentioned you might need a bit of a hand?'

Lou nodded and then pulled a face. 'I do... and it's probably more than "a bit". It's a total mess and I've got no idea where to start. I keep trimming at the edges, but the garden's definitely winning the war!'

'Maybe I could come and have a look for myself?' said Sean, 'I mean... only when it's convenient for you.'

Lou smiled at him. The poor bloke looked decidedly uncomfortable and was obviously more than aware that he'd just invited himself to her home.

'Of course!' she said, wanting to let him off the hook as quickly as possible. 'That would be brilliant!'

She was just grateful that he was up for giving her a hand at all – even if that was just in the shape of some advice on how to start in a way that would help her beat back the green wall that seemed intent on creeping up on her little cottage.

'Great,' said Sean looking relieved. 'Okay – well, that's great. Sorry… I've got somewhere I need to be now – but would tomorrow work for you? Late morning'

'Perfect!' said Lou. She wasn't back in here with Kate for a few days, and her shift at Pebble Street was in the evening. 'Erm… you know where I am?' she added.

She knew that Sean was aware of the cottage, having seen him wander past several times, but she wasn't certain that he knew it was her place.

'Yeah! You bought Shell Cottage just below the allotments, right?' he said.

'That's me,' Lou nodded.

'Can I ask… when you first moved here, weren't you renting that lovely little blue and white place just over the brow from where you are now?'

Lou raised her eyebrows in surprise. Okay – so he knew far more about her than she would have guessed.

'Sorry – you don't have to answer that!' he laughed. 'You don't know anything about me. I was just wondering why you moved such a short distance, that was all!'

'Oh!' laughed Lou, 'well… that's no secret. I needed somewhere last minute to rent – and Lizzie – my old landlady and I share a mutual friend. She let me have the place as long as I was happy with it as it was.'

'Didn't it work out?' said Sean.

'Nothing like that, thank heavens,' said Lou. 'Her place was immaculate, but I knew from the start it was going to be a short-term rental. I loved it there – and Lizzie was very open that she was either going to sell up or move back in the near future.'

'Oh!' said Sean. 'Fair enough. And… is it on the market now then?'

Lou shook her head. 'Nah – Lizzie's decided to come back to Seabury. I think she'll be in before the end of the summer.'

'Bummer for you though!' said Sean.

'Nah – not really,' Lou shrugged. 'It was gorgeous – but even if she'd sold up, it would have been well above my price range. Then I discovered Shell cottage…'

'And it was love at first sight?' said Sean.

Lou could swear she could feel the ears of the surrounding Chilly Dippers pricking up at those words. Damn – there were going to be some rumours flying around this week!

'The view is amazing,' she said, tilting her head.

LAUGHTER AND HAPPY EVER AFTER IN SEABURY

'And I really wanted to stay in Seabury. The estate agent described it as "charmingly rustic."'

'Uh oh!' laughed Sean.

'Yeah... exactly,' said Lou. 'Put it like this – I've had lots of practise with a paint roller and wallpaper stripper! It's starting to feel like home now though... it's quite small but there's only me so...' Lou trailed off. She was aware that she was on dangerous territory all of a sudden. She didn't want to sound desperate... or like a hermit... or weird... or...

Argh!

This man was making her overthink for Britain.

'It's perfect,' she finished clumsily. 'Or it will be when I've tackled the garden. I think that'll help make the place feel a bit bigger. It's like being hemmed in by a big green wall at the moment!'

'I noticed the brambles were getting a good hold back there last time I came past,' Sean nodded.

'Oh... you know the place?' said Lou lightly. She didn't want to sound like she'd been spying on him.

'Yeah,' he said wrinkling his nose in adorable discomfort, 'I mean, I've often thought of giving you a wave... but as we've never really met before I thought that might be a bit odd.'

'Next time, you'll have to stop for a cuppa!' she said, and then instantly wanted to smack herself in the face. Why did she have to be such a knob around cute men?! She was sure she wasn't this idiotic when she was chatting with her customers in here and at the hotel – so why was she tying herself up in knots.

Sean pulled his phone out of his pocket and glanced at the screen.

'Sorry Lou – I've got to go, I'm meeting someone,' he said after checking the time. He quickly downed the rest of his coffee and got to his feet – promptly drawing the eyes of everyone in the café. 'See you tomorrow?'

'Yup. See you then,' Lou nodded.

He headed straight for the door, smiling and nodding as the others yelled a volley of goodbyes and thanks for their drinks. Lou sat still, not daring to turn and watch him leave – she didn't want to give the others any more ammo than they already had.

Scrunching up her face, Lou stared down into her half-finished soup. Why did that somehow feel like the biggest anti-climax known to mankind?! What had she been expecting – a kiss on the cheek or something? That would have been completely inappropriate – after all, they'd only just met and had just been organising work on her garden. It wasn't a date. It was business... and it was her fault it had started out so awkwardly!

'Well done, Lou,' said Doris from behind her.

'Huh?' said Lou, turning around in a bit of a daze.

'Meeting up again tomorrow?' she said wiggling her eyebrows. 'Fast work. I knew I should have tried drowning the man weeks ago!'

The others roared with laughter, and Lou quickly

gave up trying to set them right. There hadn't been an ounce of flirting... but there wasn't any point telling the Dippers that. They wouldn't be interested in the fact it had been purely business – that the man was just coming to sort out her garden for her. Thank heavens he *hadn't* kissed her on the cheek – this lot would have had them married off by the end of next week otherwise.

Lou sighed, toying with the dregs of her soup. She had a lot to do before she could restart her day. She needed to get home and have a shower to wash off all the salt. She needed to comb the seaweed out of her hair too... and put on some clean clothes so that she didn't look quite so much like a salty bag lady.

Pulling herself to her feet, Lou nudged the snoozing Stanley gently away so that she could manoeuvre her way past him. That's when she spotted a pair of swimming goggles on the floor just underneath Sean's recently vacated chair. He must have dropped them.

Bending down to scoop them up, Lou laughed as Stanley got to his feet and stuck a snuffling wet nose in her ear.

'Thanks for saving me, boy!' she smiled, ruffling his wet fur. 'I'll see you tomorrow afternoon, okay?' Then, she quickly grabbed the crust of bread left on her plate and fed it to him. 'Don't tell your mum!' she whispered.

'Off to meet your lover?' said Doris, as Lou passed her chair.

Lou promptly popped Sean's goggles in her

cardigan pocket out of sight and shook her head. She had been about to ask the gaggle of troublemakers where he lived so that she could take them back to him... but there was no way she was going to do that now!

'Nah – I've got a hot date with a wallpaper scraper!' she said to the expectant faces.

'No fun!' laughed Sally. 'Well, if you decide you don't want the merman, let me know. I quite like the look of him in those swimming shorts.'

The giggling and chattering started up again, and Lou decided to make a break for it. She'd normally hang out a lot longer after a swim, getting her own fill of giggling gossip – but she hated being the centre of attention.

'Catch you all next time!' she said, then scuttled towards the door without looking back.

CHAPTER 5

Lou managed to make it all the way back to Shell Cottage without bumping into a single living soul. Seabury was deserted – it looked like she'd left everyone packed into The Sardine!

She couldn't help but feel a bit bad for ducking out so soon after the other Dippers had arrived – after all, her weekly post-swim catchups were her main source of local gossip. But this morning, she had a feeling her impromptu breakfast with Sean might just be the hottest piece of gossip in town... and she didn't much fancy fending off the good-natured jibes while she sat there steaming, covered in salt and seaweed.

Besides, there was nothing much to tell, was there? Not really. She'd just tried to drown the poor guy while asking for his help in her garden. That was it. They didn't need to know that there was something about Sean's steady gaze that made her tingle all over – and there was no way she'd be mentioning the fact that the touch of his smooth skin against hers when the waves dumped her into his arms had made her feel like a human soda-stream.

Anyway – Lou had a mission in mind, and she wasn't going to be able to stop fidgeting until she'd seen it through. She fingered the pair of goggles in her cardigan pocket. They were the perfect excuse to do a little bit of investigating of her own. After all – Sean had seen her home – she wanted a glimpse of his!

Sean had said he was off to meet someone, so it was a fairly safe bet she'd be able to get a good, undisturbed look at where he lived – from outside, of course – before leaving his goggles dangling from his doorknob. Maybe his house would tell her a bit more about this gorgeous Paths and Sheds committee member that seemed to have her on the hop! First things first, though – she was going to have a shower.

Lou was slightly breathless by the time she reached her front door. Letting herself into the silent space, she kicked off her wellingtons, leaving them in a heap in the empty hallway, and ran straight up the narrow steps to the bathroom.

'Urgh!'

The moment she caught sight of herself in the bathroom mirror, Lou regretted looking. She should have just hopped straight into her lovely pink bathtub and turned the shower on – at least that way she would have remained blissfully unaware of the total state she was in.

Lou was coated in a fine layer of sand, topped off with more seaweed than she'd thought possible. It might sound all cutesy and slightly mermaid-ish, but in reality, she looked more like a demon from the deep! Had she really sat across from Sean, chatting away with a great big slimy sliver of greeny-brown weed attached to her face?

Oh – the shame!

Reaching up, she peeled it off and flicked it into the sink. Maybe it was best not to think about it too much. She'd just jump in the shower and wash away the evidence. After all – what did it matter? It wasn't like it had been a date - she'd just been asking the man for help with her garden… after almost drowning him!

Lou got the water running and, doing her best not to catch another glimpse of herself in the mirror, clambered under the torrent. One thing she could say for her new home – it certainly had good water pressure!

The scalding hot water made her squeal and dance around, doing her best to avoid the insistent jets as they pelted her from above. It was a bit like that first hit of freezing sea water but in reverse – and it didn't take long to settle into the sensation.

As Lou's muscles started to melt, letting go of all the tension and shock of the morning, her mind flew back to the moment she'd found herself washed into Sean's unsuspecting arms. He'd held her close, doing his best to shield her from the full force of the sea as she'd coughed and spluttered into his chest.

Lou couldn't help but grin, even as she squirmed with the re-lived embarrassment of the moment. The whole thing was only just starting to unscramble in her head - it had happened so quickly. Still, there was no getting away from the fact that she'd ended up on top of him, practically naked. She gave a little shudder – half horror, half delight.

There was no getting away from the fact that this was the first time she'd felt like this since she'd walked out on her cheating turd of an ex. After Brendan, Lou had thought that part of her – the one that got all giddy over a cute guy - had switched off for good. But as the hot water continued to sluice over her, she had to admit that the images of Sean in his swimming shorts were definitely causing feelings that were far from platonic.

Why did it have to happen when she was all bedraggled and coughing and covered in seaweed though? She could think of several nicer ways to enjoy her first cuddle since Brendan… like on her sofa, or maybe in a beautifully manicured garden with a gentle breeze blowing in from the sea and then his arms could be around her and…

Lou shook her head, snapping herself out of the daydream. What was she thinking? Her imagination was starting to run away with her again. Perhaps it was time to turn the cold water up!

Shaking her head, she stared down into the bath – which was now speckled with bits of seaweed and a good coating of sand. Even over on pebble-covered North Beach, there was plenty of sand below the low tide mark that got stirred up by the waves. Gah – she must have looked a right state – both in the water and out of it. Talk about an awful first impression. The swimming cap covered in garish flowers hardly helped matters. She didn't even know what the flowers were meant to be... marigolds... or carnations... or roses?

Lou sighed. She knew nothing about gardening, or flowers, or growing things. Her and Sean clearly had nothing in common... and needed to get these silly daydreams of him out of her head. She was single... and happy to remain so.

Still – that didn't mean she couldn't accept his help with the garden, did it? And maybe she could learn a bit about plants so she didn't feel like such an idiot. She wasn't completely useless – she'd just never needed to know before, that was all. Yes... she'd ask him to teach her a bit about plants. That should provide a nice, safe topic that should stop her dribbling over the poor guy.

Right – it was time to get out, get dry... and preferably get a grip!

Hauling herself over the edge of the bathtub, Lou glanced at herself in the mirror and was relieved to see that she no longer resembled a weed-speckled sea monster. Why couldn't she have looked more like this when she'd ended up in Sean's arms? Preferably with the addition of a bit of lip-gloss, and waterproof mascara, and without her idiotic swim cap! Even so, she couldn't deny that it had been rather nice having a practically naked man rubbing against her – even if they were both basically drowning at the time.

'Quit it!' she growled at her reflection.

Blimey – she'd never got like this with Brendan... not for the last few years, anyway. He'd simply been too disapproving of her mere existence for her to dare show anything resembling attraction... or even affection.

Lou frowned as she wandered through into her bedroom, towelling herself dry rather more vigorously than was strictly necessary. It really was amazing how much clearer everything became from outside a relationship. It was obvious now that she should have left Brendan way before... before... *she* happened. Maybe she should be grateful? That said, Lou didn't much fancy having to come face-to-face with a naked teenager in her bed every time she needed a life lesson!

If she was being completely honest with herself, Lou knew she was only just coming to terms with the fact she'd wasted so many years on a relationship that had given her nothing in return... at least, nothing good! Considering all that, it was amazing how hard it was proving to get over it. Brendan still had an annoyingly strong hold on her day-to-day life. The problem was – she'd still loved him at the end. As stupid as that sounded, his betrayal had hurt her more than she'd admitted to anyone.

Well, there was no point thinking about that now, was there? It was all well and truly over. Maybe she *should* start thinking about a new relationship? Her body was certainly telling her that it was time – even if her head was struggling to catch up.

'Seriously – focus!' she groaned, realising that she was now wandering around the cramped bedroom wearing one sock, a pair of pants and nothing else.

Lou didn't usually give a second thought to what she was wearing – as long as she was comfortable, warm and able to do whatever jobs she had lined up for the day ahead, that was as far as her sartorial decisions went. Right now, though, she didn't seem to be able to make a decision about anything.

'You're just returning a pair of goggles, dumbass,' she sighed.

And he's not even going to be there!

But, on the off-chance she might bump into Sean during her mission, Lou was determined to leave him with a better impression this time. She didn't really know why she was worrying about it so much – that morning's sea-weed-coated disaster wasn't going to be hard to beat!

Lou turned to stare at the bed where there was already a pile of discarded outfits.

'Oh for goodness sake!' she groaned, picking up a

silk tee shirt, pulling a face, and promptly chucking it back on the bed in disgust.

Maybe she should just shove on her favourite pair of jeans and a warm jumper and call it quits.

Promptly ignoring her own advice, she picked up a little black dress and held it up against herself, before rolling her eyes.

Gah!

Why did she have to make everything so damn complicated?!

CHAPTER 6

At long last, Lou was dried and dressed. To make up for the fact that she'd given in and climbed into her comfy old jeans and sweater combo – she was wearing a bit of make-up for the first time in what felt like forever. But *only* because she wanted to – it had nothing at all to do with Sean and her little mission to check out his house!

Anyway, now that she'd added a bit of mascara and a slick of tinted lip-gloss to stop her lips from looking dry after all that salt water – she was almost guaranteed *not* to run into him, wasn't she?!

Letting herself out of her house, Lou strode up the little lane that led away from Shell Cottage for the second time that morning. Of course, she had no idea where to find Sean's house, so she turned her steps back towards town again. With any luck, she'd bump into someone who knew where he lived – preferably not one of the Chilly Dippers though!

Lou had a plan. If she didn't happen to meet anyone useful on her way down the hill into Seabury, she was going to drop into the hotel to see Hattie. Her excuse was that she wanted to jot down her rota for the rest of the week - even though she already knew her shift pattern off by heart. Still, it would give her a chance to grill her friend for information.

Hattie knew everyone up at the allotments - after all, they tended to turn up almost every day with a seemingly endless supply of beautifully grown fresh produce - which Hattie bought with glee. She'd developed a slightly alarming habit of creating specials on a whim and adding them to the menu with mere minutes to go before service started.

I can't help it, Loulou! she'd gushed last time Lou had tutted at having to memorise the fourth new special that week. *The vegetables just speak to me! They inspire me!* And then the pair of them had broken down in a fit of giggles at the usually down-to-earth Hattie waxing so lyrical about a crate of sugar-snap peas!

At least it meant that her best friend was almost guaranteed to know Sean – and there was a good chance she'd know where his house was, too. If not, Hattie could always ask Ben for her. He knew everyone and everywhere in Seabury – having done some kind of work in most of the properties in a five-mile radius.

As it was, Lou was saved from having to press her

grand plan into action. The moment she reached the seafront road, Ethel appeared, heading towards her at speed.

'Hello!' said Lou with a smile. She adored this woman – Ethel had shown her so much kindness when she'd first come to town – and now she felt more like a treasured member of the family rather than someone she just happened to work with.

'Lou! Hello dearie! I'm just off up to the allotments to find Charlie. Silly man left his packed lunch on the table again,' she huffed. 'Not that I mind,' she added with a soft smile, 'it means I get to spend more time with him.'

'Maybe he does it on purpose – just so he can lure you up to his shed!' said Lou, wiggling her eyebrows.

'Oh hush, you!' said Ethel, turning a very fetching shade of pink. 'You look nice, by the way – going somewhere special?'

Lou shook her head. 'Nope – Sean left his goggles in The Sardine earlier. I just wanted to return them to him.'

'Right,' said Ethel. 'That's nice.'

Lou noticed that her friend was keeping a very determined straight face, but there was definitely a twinkle in Ethel's eye! Ah well – it didn't matter – she didn't mind providing Ethel with a bit of gentle entertainment. She hadn't much liked being the centre of attention with the Chilly Dippers earlier, but Ethel was a different matter. Lou trusted Ethel completely, and had probably shown her more of her true nature than anyone else in Seabury since she'd arrived. In fact – come to think of it, she was the perfect person to ask!

'Before you go – you don't happen to know where Sean's house is do you?' she said. 'I mean – I know he's not going to be in because he said he was meeting someone, but I figured I could hang his goggles from his door handle or something!'

'Of course!' Ethel nodded. She was definitely giving her a knowing smile now. 'He's over on Sand Piper Lane.'

It wasn't a road Lou was familiar with. She might have lived in Seabury for over a year – and it might be a relatively small town - but there were tiny, winding roads and cobbled alleyways dotted all over the place. In fact, she had a feeling she could live here for her entire life and still not manage to explore every inch of it. She listened closely as Ethel gave her directions.

It wasn't long before the pair of them said goodbye and Lou was off on the hunt again. No – that *wasn't* the way she was meant to be thinking about her little mission, was it?! She was just returning the poor guy's swimming goggles, that was all!

Doing her best to ignore the fact that she could just hand them back to Sean when he came over to look at her garden in the morning, Lou delved into the back streets of Seabury. She was *sure* it was best that Sean had his goggles back today… otherwise, what would happen if he fancied an evening swim to make up for the fact that she'd ruined his morning one? He wouldn't be able to go - and it would be all her fault.

Lou wandered along, admiring the beauty of Seabury's tiny, hidden front gardens and little lanes as she went. If only she knew what some of these beautiful plants were, she'd be making lists of what she wanted in her own garden when they'd managed to tame it a bit. As it was, she simply made a mental note to wander back this way when she had a bit more time. Then she'd snap a few photos of the frothy purples, fresh whites and sweet pinks that were dancing in the gentle sea air.

It didn't take her long to find Sand Piper Lane. According to Ethel, she needed to look for number nine. The garden belonging to the house right in front of her looked pretty similar to her own. It was completely overgrown and covered in weeds which were being throttled by long, prickly runners just for good measure.

Directly in front of the house stood a bed full of leggy plants she didn't know the names of – but she'd hazard a guess they'd be more at home on a compost heap rather than running rampant all over the front garden.

Hopefully this *wasn't* Sean's place – because if this was his level of gardening prowess, she'd definitely be better going it alone after all! It couldn't be though, could it?! There was no way someone on the Paths and Sheds committee at the allotments would let his front garden get in such a state. Peering at the tarnished brass number on the front door, she let out a long sigh of relief. Number thirty-four. Phew!

Lou moved further along the lane until the next garden came into view. She came to a halt as a cold chill trickled down her spine. This poor garden had been completely paved over with ugly, grey concrete slabs – reminding her forcefully of Brendan's approach to landscaping.

There were a few concrete planters that had been placed like barricades along the front path, with just a few dead stalks poking out of the cracked, depleted soil inside. The only hint of green in the whole garden was added by the dandelions that had managed to punch their way up through the cracks in the path. Even Lou knew a dandelion when she saw one… see – she did know *something* about gardening after all!

Hopefully this wasn't the place she was looking for either. If it was, she'd have to have very stern words with her treacherous libido – there was no way she'd allow herself to fancy the pants off anyone who covered their garden with concrete. Once in a lifetime was more than enough!

Holding her breath, Lou glanced at the door.
Number four.

'Thank goodness for that!' she muttered. Clearly, the numbers on this road made zero logical sense.

Hurrying past the depressing grey tones of the concrete garden, she spotted the next gate a little further along on the other side of the lane. This one fronted an immaculate plot. It was trimmed and snipped to within an inch of its life. This one really *did* look like it might be the work of someone who belonged to a committee at the allotments… but once again, it would be a deal breaker for her less than honourable intentions if this turned out to be Sean's garden! The hedge was perfectly pruned… into the shape of a steam train.

Lou let out an involuntary giggle and then clamped her hand over her mouth. She stared around the rest of the garden, her eyes jumping from one piece of railway memorabilia to the next. There were station names screwed to the fences, and a huge carriage lamp graced the wall over the front door. She was convinced she could hear a model railway set zipping around in the loft. Luckily, this was number seventeen.

Thank goodness! This was like playing horticultural Russian roulette!

The next garden was lovely in its ordinariness. It wasn't anything particularly special – but it wasn't overgrown… or paved… or pruned using a slide rule. It was simple and uncluttered, with some bright and pretty plants waving frothily at her from the borders, along with a few planters that looked like they were still waiting to be filled. Somehow, Lou knew she'd arrived at her destination. Glancing over at the door just to make sure, she spotted the number nine she'd been looking for.

Letting herself through the wide gate, Lou was about to head along the path that led up the side of the garden when she paused. Something ahead of her had just caught her attention, and she stared hard at the side of the house.

From where she was standing, Lou could see straight along the path that led towards what must be Sean's back garden. There was... *something*... stacked against the side of the house.

Glancing up at the front windows just to make sure no one was watching her, Lou walked hastily up the path so she could get a better look.

Oh! It wasn't half as interesting as she'd been hoping. It was just a bunch of fencing panels after all.

She paused again.

No... not fencing panels. They might be stacked neatly – but they were all different colours and sizes... and some of them even had windows in them.

What on earth?!

These weren't fencing panels – they were bits of shed. Old, dismantled shed... or "sheds" she should say, as there were clearly dozens of them!

Lou frowned and turned around to look at the rest of the garden again. This time, she noticed the rolls of roofing felt stacked inside the little log shelter next to the front door. The tin bucket she'd originally taken as an empty planter was actually full of old padlocks and door hinges. Tucked behind it was a crate full of latches.

In fact, the entire garden was like a very organised graveyard for sheds – and now she knew what she was looking for, she started to spot more and more bits and pieces stacked amongst the plants. It was all neat and tidy... but the stuff was everywhere!

The sound of a distant engine brought Lou back to her senses. She was standing at the side of Sean's house having a damn good snoop... and as much as she'd love to take a quick peep at the back garden too, she'd really rather not get caught in the act.

Lou hurried over towards Sean's front door, side-eyeing the bucket of padlocks as she went. Grabbing the goggles out of her pocket, she dangled them from the handle. There. Mission accomplished. It was time to get out of here.

CHAPTER 7

Okay – so the weird shed bits and pieces were definitely a conundrum! Lou had just reached the gate when she realised that she was here unannounced, and her curiosity had led her around the side of Sean's house, uninvited.

Feeling guilty as well as mildly perturbed, she scuttled back to the front door and rang the bell. There – that was more like it… the socially acceptable thing to do rather than snooping around the garden of a relative stranger! Sure – she probably should have done that first, but hey, better late than never, right?

After a few seconds of complete silence, Lou rang the doorbell again just for good measure. Nope – clearly Sean was still out… or maybe he was upstairs lounging around in the bath, naked.

The word "naked" stuck in her head… and was that a blush?!

Why – stupid brain – why?!

She glanced down at Sean's goggles, dangling from the front door handle. Maybe she should leave him a note to explain where they'd appeared from? But she didn't have any paper… or a pen… or any idea what to write, come to that.

'Pull yourself together!' she muttered. It was time to get back to reality and get on with her day. There would be plenty of opportunities to carry on making a total tit out of herself when Sean came around to the cottage in the morning!

She was just heading back down the garden path, casting one quick, curious glance over her shoulder and the pile of shed panels, when the loud rumble of an approaching vehicle met her ears.

Lou hurried towards the gate, only for Sean to pull up next to her in a battered old truck with a trailer attached to the back. She gaped at it, her mouth open wide in surprise.

Strapped to the trailer with every bit of manky old rope Seabury must possess, was the most ramshackle-looking shed Lou had ever seen. It had a corrugated, iron roof that was more rust than metal. The side facing her had a single window that appeared to have come from something else - it was made from bright, stained glass. A couple of the little panes were cracked, and a few pieces were missing completely. It looked a bit bizarre surrounded by the rest of the shed.

As Sean hit the brakes and the trailer came to a

bumping halt, Lou noticed a rusty old kettle swinging from a hook outside the shed's old door. She wondered how on earth he'd had managed to get the whole thing onto the trailer in one piece – let alone drive it all the way back to his house without it falling apart en route!

Sean was grinning at her in delight, and the minute Lou caught his eye, something in her chest did a funny squeezy-popping motion.

What on earth?!

'Like my little find?' he called cheerfully as he hopped out of the car. 'Isn't she a beauty?!'

'Erm... sure?' said Lou.

She wasn't really sure what she was meant to say. It looked to her like he'd had taken a wrong turn on the way to the tip – surely he hadn't meant to bring this rusty old heap back home with him?

'Do you need a hand getting it down or something?' she said, doing her best to sound helpful, though she'd just crossed her fingers in her pocket that the answer would be *no!*

'Nah – thanks though!' said Sean, shaking his head. 'I've got a friend with a tractor who's turning up a bit later on to help me unload.'

'Right!' said Lou, with an internal sigh of relief.

If she was honest, she very much doubted that shed was going to still be in one piece by the time Sean had got it down from there. In fact... it looked like it was ready to disintegrate the minute someone untied those ropes!

'I know it doesn't look like much,' said Sean, chuckling at the sceptical look Lou hadn't managed to keep off her face, 'but there's some useful timber in there – and that gorgeous window can definitely be used again... I think... I mean, I'm not entirely sure – those little panes probably need repairing.'

Lou nodded along in complete confusion. Most people hid their weirdnesses, their obsessions and freak flags. It usually took weeks, months... or even years... to discover the little idiosyncrasies that made people tick. That clearly wasn't the case with Sean, though!

'Anyway,' he continued, 'it didn't cost me anything, and the farmer was going to bung the whole thing on a bonfire if I didn't collect it today.'

'A bonfire?' echoed Lou. She wasn't about to tell Sean, but she couldn't help secretly agreeing with the farmer that it was probably the best place for it.

'I know!' said Sean, looking wide-eyed and scandalised. 'He had his crowbar, chainsaw and a box of matches at the ready. I think I only just got there in time to stop him pouring the oil from an old paraffin lamp over the poor old thing and setting it alight!'

'Blimey!' said Lou.

'Right?!' he gasped. 'I actually need to thank you for clonking into me this morning... otherwise, I'd have been swimming for a lot longer and the whole thing would have gone up in smoke.'

'Oh,' said Lou, having to bite her lip now to stop

herself from giggling. Today was getting weirder by the second. In her opinion, starting the day *without* a bump on your head and *without* a knackered old shed on a trailer sitting outside your house was probably a better outcome – but each to their own! 'Erm... what are you going to do with it?'

It wasn't as though he could use it as an actual shed, was it?! The first gust of wind that blew up from the sea would turn it into a pile of rusty metal and shards of brightly coloured glass with an old kettle on top!

'I'll take it apart and make something else out of it!' said Sean with a wide, excited grin.

'You will?' said Lou doubtfully, tearing her eyes away from his beaming face to stare at the pile of rust again. The only bits of wood she could see were rotten and covered in moss. 'Like... a bookshelf?' she said doubtfully. There wasn't much there he could use, surely? 'Or... bookends? Or a trinket box?'

'Much bigger than that!' laughed Sean. 'Come with me – I'll show you!'

'Oh... erm, okay. By the way – I came to return your goggles,' she said, suddenly feeling like she needed to explain why she was loitering in his front garden... not that he seemed to mind in the slightest! She pointed to where they were hanging from his front door handle.

'Brilliant – thank you,' said Sean. 'I was wondering where I'd left those... though they usually turn up somewhere. Come on – follow me!'

Grabbing her hand and almost making her heart jump right out of her chest, Sean led the way back up his garden path and around the side of the house. Lou picked her way past the stack of shed panels and then followed him through a wooden gate into his back garden.

She stopped dead, her mouth open in surprise.

Absolutely nothing could have prepared her for the wonderland she'd just wandered into. She was standing in a tiny village – surrounded by little houses. Well... maybe *little* wasn't exactly the right word to describe some of them. She stared around, picking out the recycled bits of shed... and boat oars... and bannisters...

Sean had built a village of perfect, beautiful houses – but in miniature. Lou felt like a giant standing inside a fairy tale. Off to the right were a couple of houses that looked like they were still in the process of being built.

'Be my guest!' said Sean, clearly noticing her curious stare in that direction.

Lou, who'd been rooted to the spot in complete surprise, finally managed to move. She nodded and, still in a bit of a daze, wandered over towards one of the half-built houses, staring at it in wonder. Okay, so they weren't just for show. They were clearly built with a lot of love, and were works of art in their own right – but this one also had more mod-cons than her own cottage!

'I'm about to put the wood burner in this one,' said

Sean, coming to stand next to her and pointing at a hearth in the corner, and a flue pipe that led up and out of the roof. 'I've just finished the electrics on this one,' he added, moving three doors down.

Reaching in and around the corner, he flicked a switch and Lou gasped as warm, honeyed light shone from the two round windows.

'They're amazing!' said Lou in wide-eyed wonder. 'When can I move in?'

Sean beamed at her. 'See – this is what I collect the old sheds for! Everything here has been built from scrap I've picked up from people's fields and gardens.'

'I'm... I... wow!' said Lou, turning to stare along the line of houses on the other side of the garden. She was speechless - not something that happened very often, she had to admit. 'They're really all from old sheds?'

'Sheds... beach huts... boat houses... that sort of thing,' Sean nodded. 'I can't stand seeing an old shed go to waste, so I re-make them into something else!'

'What on earth are you going to do when your garden's full?' laughed Lou.

As far as she could see, he was coming dangerously close to that happening already. His back garden was surprisingly large, but with what must be twenty or so little houses out here, he was in danger of running out of room any time soon.

'Ah – no need to worry about that,' laughed Sean. 'They tend to find new homes whenever I need the space to start a new one.'

'If I was you, I'd never want to see them leave!' said Lou.

'I love it when they go,' Sean shrugged. 'Then they get a new lease of life as a space someone loves to hang out in. People use them as garden rooms, or offices, or somewhere for kids to play. They might be small, but they're lovely and cosy. I know I'm a bit biased, but I think they have a kind of spirit to them… like they're glad of a second chance to shine.'

He shot her a slightly sheepish smile. Lou smiled back, nodding. She could see exactly what he meant – and felt quite honoured that he'd just shared it with her.

Blimey – there really wasn't any telling the kind of talent that people hid in their back gardens, was there?

CHAPTER 8

'Okay, Loulou – spill!' said Hattie, stepping back from the oven having loaded in two beautifully risen loaves.

'Spill what?!' said Lou through a mouthful of Pebble Street pudding.

Hattie had placed the enormous metal baking tray in front of her and then handed her a spoon without bothering to ask if she wanted to clean up the crumbs. Hattie and Lou may not have been best friends for that long, but Hattie definitely knew how to put a smile on her face. Unfortunately, she also seemed to know when Lou was hiding something.

'Don't give me that,' said Hattie, narrowing her eyes. 'You've been a dithering mess all afternoon – it's not like you.'

'Have not,' muttered Lou through a packed face full of pudding.

'Have too! I've literally never known you to deliver the wrong food to the wrong tables before,' said Hattie.

Lou looked at her friend in horror. 'I didn't, did I?'

Hattie nodded. 'Twice!' she said. 'Lionel sorted it out – no harm done.'

'I'm so sorry!' gasped Lou. Suddenly, her appetite for the pudding scrapings seemed to have disappeared, and she dropped her spoon with a clang.

'Seriously – there's no need to apologise,' said Hattie, meeting her eye. 'I'm just worried about you, that's all! Is everything okay?'

Lou swallowed her last mouthful of pudding with difficulty. It seemed to be lodged in her throat with a lump of emotion the size of a cricket ball. Hot tears sprang to her eyes, and she hastily tried to blink them away.

Gah! Could she get any more embarrassing?!

Hattie might be her best friend – but she was also her boss, and they were at work – she needed to get a grip!

'Oh God!' said Hattie, hurrying to her side and patting her awkwardly on the shoulder. 'Now you've got me really worried!'

'Don't be!' muttered Lou. 'I'm just being a total drama banana, that's all.'

'Come on,' said Hattie, 'you know me better than that. I'm basically going to keep bugging you until you tell me what's wrong, so you may as well save us both an awful lot of time and effort.'

Lou couldn't help but smirk at that.

'Okay... fine,' she sighed. 'But... you've got to keep it to yourself, okay? And you've got to keep a straight face.'

'Scout's honour!' said Hattie, clearly biting the inside of her cheeks in preparation.

'Man, this is embarrassing,' muttered Lou. 'Especially at my age!'

'Get on with it!' said Hattie.

'Fine,' sighed Lou. 'I've got a crush, okay!'

'Witterwoo!' said Hattie, instantly reverting to primary-school mode. 'Wow – I was *not* expecting that!'

Lou just pulled a face.

'Why the face?' demanded Hattie. 'Are they married... or... don't they like you... or...?'

'I basically don't know anything about him,' said Hattie, her voice wobbling. 'Plus, it's really bloody inconvenient considering I've sworn off relationships forever.'

'Okay – first things first,' said Hattie, pulling a stool up opposite Lou at the kitchen island and perching on it. 'Who is the mystery man?'

'Sean,' Lou muttered, covering her eyes as if that would make it all go away.

'Swimming Sean?' said Hattie, her eyebrows raised. 'Paths and Sheds Sean?'

'Are there any other Seans in town?' said Lou.

'I don't think so,' said Hattie. 'Just checking. And,

just for the record, I can totally see why you fancy him. I mean - don't tell Ben I said this – but that man knows how to wear a pair of swimming shorts, doesn't he?!'

Lou nodded, blushing as memories of their skin-on-skin collision poked her in the brain.

'And why the epic, awkward blush there?' demanded Hattie.

'Because I basically made the biggest arse out of myself while he was wearing said swimming shorts!' said Lou, leaning her head in her hands so that she didn't have to look at Hattie, who was now grinning at her.

'What did you do,' she said

Lou could hear the barely concealed laughter in her friend's voice.

'I wanted to talk to him about helping me in the garden,' said Lou. 'Charlie suggested him.'

'Good choice,' said Hattie. 'Though why you don't just ask Ben is beyond me!'

'Because I figured you might actually like to see your own boyfriend one of these days in between his three thousand jobs?' said Lou.

'Oh right!' laughed Hattie. 'That!'

'So anyway… I swam after him…. Sean, I mean.'

'Of *course* you did!' chuckled Hattie. 'Paint me a picture here – were you wearing your flowery cap?'

Lou nodded with a pout. 'And my baggy costume.'

'Classic!' giggled Hattie.

'Sean went under, and I thought he was drowning,'

said Lou with a slight shudder as the embarrassment washed over her in a fresh wave of humiliation.

Hattie was giggling, as if she knew the story was going to have a disastrous ending. 'And?!' she demanded.

'I bashed into him. Face first. And then... well... we both came up spluttering and I was all over him and…. GAH!'

Hattie snorted, and Lou grimaced at her. 'Don't – it was awful!'

'How awful?'

Lou shrugged.

'It can't have been that bad,' said Hattie. 'From what I know of Sean, he seems pretty chilled.'

'He was lovely,' said Lou with a sigh. 'After we'd spat out all the salt water and Stanley had tried to save us both, we had coffee in The Sardine. Then I went to his house.'

'Wait... what?!' said Lou. 'Is this turning into one of those filthy novels? You didn't shower together and-'

'NO!' squeaked Lou. 'He left his goggles at the café, so I took them over to him, that's all. And then he showed me his back garden.'

'His back garden!' hooted Hattie, slapping the counter in front of her.

'You're a *huge* support,' said Lou with a frown – though she was having to bite her lip to stop herself from joining in with Hattie's giggles.

For some reason, Lou didn't feel like telling her

about the amazing, tiny houses right now. It had been special, somehow. She'd really loved them, and she didn't want to have to defend them from Hattie's double-entendre-induced giggle fit. Especially as she didn't really know Sean. After all – he *could* still turn out to be a total weirdo with a train set in the attic!

'Okay, okay!' said Hattie, practically hiccupping herself back to sanity, 'putting aside your slightly peculiar tactics for a moment – *why* exactly are you having a meltdown about this? He seems like a nice guy. You're single. He's single…'

'He is?' gasped Lou, grabbing at the titbit of information as if it was a lifeline.

'Of course!' said Hattie. 'You've really not done your homework, have you?'

'Have too,' muttered Lou.

'Staring at his bum in his swimming costume doesn't count,' said Hattie.

Lou stuck out her bottom lip.

'So… why all the moping?' demanded Hattie again.

'I… I just… he's coming over tomorrow to help with the garden,' said Lou, as if that explained everything.

'And?!' said Hattie, sounding exasperated.

'And what if he arrives and pours concrete over half of it and paves the rest of it?!' said Lou, the words coming out in a rush.

Hattie took her hand. 'He isn't your tw…idiot of an ex,' she said gently. 'Not all men are complete bell… peppers.'

Lou twitched a little smile at that. 'I know. But... what if it goes wrong?'

'What? The garden?' said Hattie.

Lou shook her head. 'What if I really like him, and he doesn't really like me, and it all implodes and then I have to leave Seabury. I've only just bought my house!'

'Okay – you need to breathe,' said Hattie. 'And slowly.'

Lou nodded and for once in her life did as she was told.

'Nothing has to change,' said Hattie. 'You can just take some time and see if this little crush of yours hangs around...'

'If I do that, I'll lose both my jobs if today's anything to go by,' sighed Lou.

Hattie grinned. 'Nah – I think you've got a bit of leeway.'

'But... what if I don't want to wait,' said Lou – this time her voice was tiny and scared.

'Well... he's coming over to yours tomorrow, isn't he?' said Hattie.

Lou nodded, her stomach swooping at the thought.

'Well then... maybe it's time to exercise your flirting muscle, Ms Walters.'

'Nope,' said Lou decidedly. 'I haven't had to do that for nearly two decades. Besides... I don't think I was born with one.'

'Erm... what are we talking about now?' said Hattie.

'A flirting muscle!' said Lou.

'Right. Well, that's rubbish. I've seen what you're like with our diners - and when you're working over at the café.'

'What, treat the poor guy like he's just ordered a BLT?!' said Lou.

'No, dumb dumb – just be easy and bantery and yourself,' said Hattie. 'Test the waters, see if there's a spark between you.'

'Then what?' said Lou.

'Stop looking too far ahead!' said Hattie. 'Maybe... maybe just enjoy that bit for a while if it's there. Just be yourself.'

'It's never a very good plan,' sighed Lou. 'Last time I did that, I was wearing a plastic swimming cap and nearly drowned the poor guy by headbutting him in the face.'

Hattie considered her for a moment. 'Maybe a little bit less headbutting,' she conceded. 'But – it worked, didn't it? You ended up with his arms around you, you went for a coffee and he's coming to yours tomorrow.'

'You make it sound so easy,' said Lou.

'It is!' insisted Hattie. 'Just take it slow and see where it leads you.'

'What if I don't want to take it slow, though,' said Lou, looking mortified.

'Well,' said Hattie, getting to her feet and grabbing her oven mitts in preparation for pulling the two divine-smelling loaves from the oven, 'then you're simply going to have to jump on him again and hope he gets the hint!'

'What?!' said Lou, though she had to admit, the memory of their wet, salty, sandy tumble made this a far more appealing – if terrifying – option.

'What?' said Hattie with an innocent shrug. 'I need you to do whatever it takes to get your head back on your shoulders and out of the clouds. If that means you have to pounce on the poor guy – I'm happy to sacrifice him for the cause!'

Lou stuck her tongue out at Hattie, drew the baking dish back towards her and reunited herself with her spoon.

'Just promise me one thing,' said Hattie.

'What?' said Lou, getting back to scraping the edges clean.

'Just be safe,' she said with a sly wink as she bent to retrieve her buns from the oven.

CHAPTER 9

The living room at Shell Cottage really wasn't made for nervous pacing, but Lou was giving it a damn good go anyway. Unfortunately, the two-and-a-half steps it afforded her were making her feel more like a human ping-pong ball rather than helping her to release any nervous energy.

Pausing for a moment, Lou let out an irritated breath. She was annoyed with herself for being so ridiculous. She had no reason to be this worked up about Sean's arrival… but telling herself that wasn't making things any easier.

'Gah!'

She promptly resumed her rattling around. Anything was better than standing still and staring out of the window like a dog waiting for its master to return.

Sean was due at any moment. As she'd basically

been on high alert waiting for him since she'd got up – Lou had tidied the cottage to within an inch of its life. She'd cleaned and primped and polished… and what was the point? It would just be covered in flecks of old wallpaper and a layer of plaster dust again before she knew it!

Lou couldn't help it – she had to keep her hands busy somehow! By this point, things had gone from bad to ridiculous though, and she'd rearranged the magazines on her minuscule coffee table about a dozen times. She'd started by stacking them, then she'd spread them out in a fan. Then, having kicked herself for being the world's biggest idiot, she'd swept them back into a pile. Now, she was starting to obsess about which one should sit on top and what it might say about her.

'Idiot!' she muttered, rearranging them again – this time in chronological order.

Why the hell was she behaving like this?! It was so out of character, she barely recognised herself. But then, Lou had been finding out all sorts of new things about herself since she'd arrived in Seabury.

Having time alone away from Brendan and his particular brand of soul-sucking had given her a chance to just *be*. Lou knew it wasn't fair to attribute all her problems to him… after all, he hadn't been a *total* monster. In fact, she'd still loved him enough at the end that it had snapped something inside her when she'd caught him in bed with *her*.

Lou blew out a breath as the customary wave of hurt swept over her. When she was forced to tell the story to anyone, she was always careful to make sure that it was a comedy anecdote.

Haha yes, he traded me for a younger model.

Can you believe she was nineteen and had a nose piercing?

I had to move away – there's no way the poor lamb could compete with me – it wouldn't have been fair to her.

Hahahahaha!

In reality – it just hurt. A lot. The term "finding them in bed together" made it sound all fluffy and cutesy when it had been anything but. It had been gross, and sweaty, and there were images she'd never be able to get out of her head. And yet – it had been heart-breaking – but not in that bittersweet, soft-focus movie kind of way. It had felt like the safety glass in her heart had shattered, cutting her to shreds. Even now, the shards were still causing damage.

Lou swallowed hard and wrapped her arms around herself. Why had she gone down *this* rabbit hole just before Sean was about to turn up? In general, she'd been happier and a lot less tense since she'd moved to Seabury… but right now, that definitely wasn't the case!

A sudden rap on the front door made Lou jump. How on earth had he managed to sneak up on her after she'd been watching for him all morning?! She let out a long breath, desperately trying to steady herself, before dashing into the hallway. She just needed to focus on the fact that Sean was there to help her with the garden. That was all… anything else could just wait.

'Hey!' she said, forcing a smile onto her face as she yanked the front door open. Sean was standing there, beaming at her. Well… that had to be a good start. So did the fact that he'd actually turned up, even though he'd had to deal with her weirdness the day before. Even better – he hadn't done a u-turn after seeing the state of the front garden. She wondered if that would still be the case when he saw the jungle waiting for him around the back!

'Hi!' said Sean in amusement as she continued to gaze at him without saying a word.

Something seemed to settle inside Lou with that friendly little word – something warm and calm. Okay – she could do this. She could show him around the garden without having a meltdown *or* throwing herself at him.

'Come on in!' she said at last, glad to hear her voice sounding steady and about as normal as it got.

Sean shook his head.

Uh oh! Maybe she spoke too soon!

'Don't look so worried!' he laughed, pointing at his boots. 'I've just come down from the allotments and I don't want to leave footprints!'

'Right!' said Lou in relief.

Shame – it looked like her obsessive magazine organising was going to go to waste, but hey – that was probably the least of her worries right now. 'Follow me!' she said, pulling the door closed behind her and leading Sean down the passageway beside the garage.

'Oh. Blimey,' said Sean, as they drew to a halt in front of the wall of vegetation.

'You know – having the hardened gardener shocked by the state of affairs isn't particularly reassuring!' said Lou, sneaking a glance at his face.

'Sorry,' he said, returning her smile, then turning back to the mess in front of them. 'It just... doesn't look *quite* so wild from the other side of the wall. Or... quite this big!'

'There's meant to be about half an acre,' said Lou, 'though frankly, it feels tiny at the moment with all this mess.'

Sean nodded. 'It looks like it's on a bit of a hill though?'

'Yep,' said Lou. 'There's even a bit of cliff edge at the far end somewhere. I could just about see a bit of rock poking out when it was winter and everything had died down a bit... but obviously it's all run rampant since then. It's in there somewhere though... so... just don't go disappearing over the edge, okay?!'

'Okay!' said Sean, looking slightly bemused. 'Any other hazards I should know about?'

'I haven't actually seen any – but I'm betting there are probably slugs the size of Shetland ponies in there somewhere!' she said with a little shrug.

'Well... I reckon you're probably right,' Sean

laughed. 'I think we're likely to discover a few things neither of us are expecting while we're sorting this lot out!'

Lou cast another surreptitious look at him. Had there been more than one meaning behind those words, or was that just her over-fried imagination getting a bit too hopeful?

No – she had to stop thinking like that! The poor guy had just come over to help her out - it wasn't fair for her to be letching over him. Frankly, she should just be grateful to have him standing in her garden and not telling her that a load of concrete was on its way, followed by a delivery of paving slabs!

Suddenly Lou was back in her old house, being told that she had to move her car out of the way so that Brendan could "deal with the garden" – as though it was some kind of enemy. It didn't matter that it was the last thing Lou had wanted – he'd just gone ahead and throttled the life out of it under a blanket of concrete.

Lou gave an involuntary shudder. For what must have been the thousandth time since she'd escaped to Seabury, she wondered why she'd ever been so in love with that man.

Had she ever… really?

The answer had to be *yes*, because the heartbreak had been very real… it still was. But recently, she'd started to wonder whether that was more about the loss of all of those years. Maybe she was in mourning for the life that could have been... the fun she could have had. Lou was very aware she'd come close to losing her true self forever.

'Earth to Lou?' came Sean's gentle voice.

Her head snapped up, and she looked at him, wide-eyed.

'Shit – I'm sorry!' she said.

Oh god, how long had she been standing there, staring into the semi-distance, obsessing over a guy that definitely didn't deserve another second of her life wasting on him? Lou blew out a breath. She didn't seem to be able to get Brendan out of her head at the moment. She'd hoped that as time went by she'd be less angry... but the opposite seemed to be happening.

'You were miles away,' he laughed.

'Yeah,' she sighed.

'Somewhere nice?' he said.

Lou quickly shook her head. 'Trust me, it's much nicer here!'

'Ah,' said Sean.

Lou could kick herself. Talk about killing the nice, easy mood they had going on between them. Now Sean was looking around uncomfortably, clearly gutted to have put his foot in it.

'Anyway,' she said quickly, 'what were you saying?'

Sean's smile snapped straight back on again.

'I was actually just wondering if you've got any gardening stuff here? I've got a few bits in the truck, but I can always head up to the allotments and grab anything else we need!'

'Oh!' said Lou, surprised. 'You want to start now?'

'If that's okay with you?' he said, raising his eyebrows. 'I mean, it's definitely going to take a bit of doing – and it's a nice day. But – only if it's convenient?'

'Convenient?' laughed Lou. 'It'd be brilliant. And I'm pretty sure there are a few things around here somewhere. There's a spade and a fork in the garage somewhere, and a knackered old wheelbarrow that was here when I bought the place – the tyre needs inflating though.'

Lou's mind was running over all the bits and pieces she'd gathered over the years but never had the opportunity to use in the paved, concrete wasteland she used to call home.

'Erm... that's great,' laughed Sean, 'but do you have anything with a blade? I'm not sure a spade and a fork are going to quite manage this lot... unless you're planning to dig from now until next year.'

'Oh!' laughed Lou. 'I mean... not really, to be honest. Sorry.'

Sean shrugged. 'That's okay, I've got my old slash-hook with me and a couple of pairs of secateurs too. We can make a start and go from there.'

'Excellent!' said Lou. 'Actually – I've just remembered. Dad's old lawnmower's still in the shed too! I've got an old tarp over it – though I'm not sure there's much point. It never worked very well...'

She trailed off. She wasn't really sure it was such a great idea to introduce Sean to the old thing. After all, she had a feeling it was at least half the reason Brendan had become obsessed with concrete.

Lou's dad had given them the lawnmower as a moving-in present, and Brendan had gone into a sulk for weeks. Brendan and her father had never seen eye to eye. Her ex was only interested in convenience and ease, but her dad had valued looking after things with love and care - so that they'd last.

The lawnmower was from the nineteen-fifties. It was difficult to start and heavy to push around – and pretty noisy and smelly too – but Lou loved it. For her, it held precious childhood memories of her dad mixed with the scent of fresh grass and warm, sunny summer days.

Brendan had whined that he could never get it going, and he'd spent quite a bit of time kicking the living daylights out of it, swearing his head off. Then the concrete had happened.

'I've lost you again!' said Sean in concern.

'Sorry!' said Lou. 'I was just trying to remember if I'd covered it up with a tarp or not.' She knew it was a pathetic excuse – as *if* she'd risk it coming to any more harm under her watch! 'It's in the garage.'

'Lead the way!' said Sean, a note of excitement in his voice.

CHAPTER 10

Lou pulled back the tarpaulin with a flourish, before letting out a series of explosive sneezes as the dust made its way straight up her nose.

Great. Very attractive!

Thanking her lucky stars that she was in here on her own because there wasn't enough floor space amongst the piles of boxes for both of them, she quickly blew her nose. Blinking hard and trying to stem any more explosions, she pushed the heavy old machine out into the sunshine.

'Erm – bless you!' said Sean, his eyes twinkling.

'Thanks,' she said, giving him a rueful smile. It had been too much to hope he hadn't heard her – given the fact her sneezing was legendary, and loud enough to disturb everyone from here to Bucklepool! At least he'd been spared the sight of her comedy pre-sneeze faces though – that was something!

With a delicate sniff, Lou gestured down at the mower and gave a kind of one-armed shrug. Out here in the sunshine, it looked just as battered as ever. It was coated in a layer of dust despite its cover, and Lou could see all the dents where Brendan had kicked it.

She glanced at Sean, expecting to find a look of exasperation or disdain on his face. Instead, he was smiling at the old machine – definitely not something Brendan had ever done!

'It was my dad's,' she said. 'He gave it to us when we moved in together.'

'Oh,' said Sean in surprise. 'I didn't realise you'd moved here with someone.'

Lou quickly shook her head. 'Nope – no no no. I mean – it's just me now. I moved here on my own. I was talking about my ex.'

'Oh – sorry!' said Sean, his eyes on the gravel path as he scuffed his boot along the surface.

Something in the way he said it made Lou raise her eyebrows. He didn't sound *that* sorry. Curious! 'Don't worry about it,' she said. 'Anyway, the poor old thing wasn't quite so dented back then. Brendan used to like giving it a good kicking when he couldn't get it going – he was quite… impatient.'

'Right,' said Sean with a slight frown. 'When was it last running?'

'Well over ten years ago. Probably nearer twenty if I'm honest!' she said with a sheepish smile.

'Right,' said Sean again, scratching his head. 'Well – I'll take her round to the back garden and see what I can do.'

'Cool,' said Lou. 'I'll just go put the kettle on then.'

She didn't wait for him to answer – she was pretty keen to get out of the way before the fun and games started. There was no way Sean would get the old thing running – not after such a long time!

Maybe next time he came, he could bring his own mower. In fact, perhaps she shouldn't have even mentioned that old antique at all! It would have probably been better to leave it snoozing under its tarpaulin and then turn it into some kind of planter when they'd finally managed to get the garden under control.

Lou had just filled the kettle and plugged it in when she heard the mower starting to cough and grumble. Then nothing.

Uh oh!

She had to take a very purposeful deep breath to stop herself from reacting to the sound. The last time she'd heard it, Brendan had stormed in in a rage. He'd never exactly taken it out on her – but the swearing and stomping and raging had always put her on edge.

Outside on the tiny patch of cobbles, the mower started to complain again. It was making the same dry coughing sounds, followed by uncooperative silence.

Lou couldn't hear a single sound coming from Sean though.

She tiptoed towards the window and peered out. Sean was bent low over the old machine. It looked like he was chatting to it and tinkering around with some kind of tool. She couldn't really see what he was up to.

Quickly, she ducked back out of sight, reaching for a pair of mugs to make their coffee. The last thing she wanted was to get caught staring out of the kitchen window – that used to make Brendan incandescent. It would take him hours to calm down, and then he'd go on about her supposed "spying" for weeks.

He really had been a giant pain in the posterior, hadn't he?!

Lou let out a little snort as the realisation that she no longer had to deal with his ridiculousness hit her all over again.

The main problem with Brendan when it had come to any kind of DIY or household job was that he'd had a huge belief in his own abilities - when in reality the man didn't have the faintest clue what he was doing. It had never taken him long to revert to the kick-it-and-yell routine.

Sean was clearly very different. Lou peeped out of the window again, only to catch him giving the mower a fond pat before attempting to start it again. The machine started to cough – but this time it sounded a lot more enthusiastic.

Lou turned away and headed over towards the

kettle – only to hear an encouraging chug from outside, followed by a growling *whoomp*.

'No way!' she murmured, turning to stare out of the window again.

The old thing was purring like a kitten and Sean was looking a bit like a proud dad as he pushed it along the edge of the cobbles, nibbling away at the undergrowth. The scent of freshly mown grass – with a good dollop of random weeds thrown in - wafted into the kitchen. Lou grinned. If ever something smelled like hope – that was it.

Quickly making two cups of coffee, Lou threw open the back door and carried them through. She rested the mugs on a low wall and watched as Sean and the mower scythed their way through a wide stretch of grass and weeds just beyond her little patch of cobbles. Making their way steadily backwards and forwards, they hacked stripes into the undergrowth.

'Well!' said Sean with a huge grin as he finally came to a halt and let the engine die away into nothing. 'How about that!'

'I can't believe you got it going!' laughed Lou. 'Amazing!'

'She'll need some fresh oil and fuel – and she could definitely do with a service, but these things never give up!' he said, brushing grass clippings from the front of his jeans where the old machine had enthusiastically flung them up at him. 'I'm afraid that's about it for what can be mown for now though!' he laughed, staring at the high walls of weeds that loomed over the scruffy, newly cut patch.

Lou nodded and swallowed hard. She was feeling ridiculously emotional considering it was just a battered old machine – but she'd honestly thought she'd never get to see it running again. Not after all the punishment it had received from Brendan.

'Shame there isn't more lawn!' she said, her voice slightly choked

Sean shrugged. 'Just you wait until we've cleared some of that lot! You'll have manicured stripes before you know it – if you want them.'

'I've got a feeling it might take a while before we get to that point!' laughed Lou.

'Well – if you'll let me take her away with me tonight, I'll bring her back as good as new next time I come over?' said Sean easily.

Lou nodded excitedly. 'That would be amazing – thank you. Here – coffee! I'd say you've already earned it.'

Sean took the mug from her carefully before holding it out to chink it against hers.

'Cheers,' he said, his face serious.

Lou stared at him a moment, then echoed him quietly before taking a sip.

'Well – there's certainly a lot to do!' said Sean as he surveyed the garden again.

'You sure you're up for it?' said Lou. She had to be

fair, the poor guy hadn't known what he was letting himself in for when she'd accosted him in the sea.

'Absolutely!' said Sean. 'It's just my kind of project – see what we can unearth under all these weeds.'

'What can I do?' said Lou excitedly, downing her coffee and plonking her mug back on the wall. The tangle of greenery had looked like an impenetrable problem when she'd been facing it on her own, but with Sean here, it felt more like a mini garden adventure!

'Get these on for a start!' said Sean, yanking a large pair of strong gloves out of his pocket and handing them to her.

'Excellent,' said Lou, pulling them on and then grabbing a pair of secateurs that were sitting on the wall.

'Erm – nope!' said Sean. Laughing, he reached out and took the secateurs from her, swapping them for a lethal pair of sharp-looking shears.

'I had these in the truck. They should do some damage!' he said.

'Cool!' said Lou, giving them an experimental snip in the air, making Sean duck out of reach with a grin.

'Total natural,' he laughed, 'now just aim it at the unwanted green stuff!'

Lou nodded, then turned to stare at the wall of greenery. Blimey… this was going to be a job and a half. It was hard to know where to even start.

'Ready?' said Sean, gulping down the remains of his coffee.

'Honestly… I've got no idea how to even start!' said Lou with a little laugh.

'Pick a spot – and start tunnelling,' said Sean, and with his sharp hook, he began to swing it at the base of the nearest stems, slowly making his way into the undergrowth like an explorer.

Lou took a deep breath, zoned in on her own patch of greenery, and started to work.

It was seriously slow going – but weirdly, it was a lot of fun too. It wasn't long before Lou's face was tingling with heat, but she was grinning from ear to ear. She snipped away, hacking at each long, trailing sucker before yanking it from the tangled mess and chopping it into neat, short pieces on the pile behind her.

Sean had asked her whether it was okay to start a small bonfire, and the scent of cut grass and sappy smoke filled the seaside air. Lou had never felt so alive as she fed the hissing, crackling fire with her clippings. She wasn't sure anything could be better than this.

'How's the budding gardener?' asked Sean, leaning on his hook for a rest as he watched her feeding the fire.

'Erm… I'd say this is more anti-gardening, wouldn't you?' laughed Lou.

'Nah – that's what people don't realise,' said Sean with a shrug. 'A lot of gardening is actually clearing! It's important to let light and air in so that new things can grow.'

Lou felt the hairs on the back of her neck stand to attention. That's exactly what she needed, too. Light – and air – and a bit of attention. Maybe if she could shed some old wood and bad memories, she could grow some new shoots too!

'You know,' she said, 'I really want to learn more about plants. I've basically got no idea what I've been dismembering so far!'

'I can help with that,' said Sean easily.

'Cool,' said Lou. 'So... what's this?' She drew Sean's attention to a tiny plant she'd carefully chopped around in case it was something important.

'Bramble,' said Sean, clearly doing his best to keep his face straight.

'Oh, right,' said Lou, quickly using her shears to lop it off at ground level. 'And this one?' she said, pointing at another lovely green shoot. She was certain this was something exciting.

'Bramble,' said Sean again.

Lou glanced at him to check he wasn't joking, but nope.

'Damn it!' she laughed, chopping it off too.

'And this one?' she said, absolutely certain this was something more exciting.

'Bramble,' said Sean again.

'But... it... what?' stuttered Lou.

'Just kidding!' he said quickly before she had the chance to chop it off too.

Lou poked her tongue out at him and he burst out

laughing. She wriggled. He had a lovely laugh. Plus, he didn't shout at old lawnmowers that couldn't help being old... or kick them. Why couldn't she have met someone like Sean all those years ago instead of wasting so much time and getting her heart broken by an idiot?

Maybe... maybe it didn't matter. She'd met Sean now... and it was up to her to decide what she wanted to do next.

CHAPTER 11

Lou straightened up and blew out a long breath, staring out towards the sea. She was surprised to see the candy-floss-tinted clouds. The light was softer and lower heralding late afternoon – they'd been at it for hours now. She quickly checked her watch. Yup – she didn't have long before she'd need to call it quits and get ready for work… but she'd been having such a gorgeous time working next to Sean that she didn't want it to come to an end!

Pulling in a deep breath, Lou revelled in the scent of the fire mingling with fresh-cut grass and salty sea air. A blackbird was singing somewhere in the field beyond her garden wall, and for a moment, everything felt perfect and dreamy.

Lou hadn't been keen on inviting someone else into her private space – especially not when it came to helping her with something she'd "admitted defeat" on – but today with Sean had been nothing short of blissful.

They'd made a surprisingly good team. The vast wall of brambles had been cut back a long way and between then, they'd managed to get the long strands of the honeysuckle she'd discovered under control. They'd even discovered several huge rhododendrons in the mess. Sean's sharp hook had carved great swathes into the patches of brambles surrounding them and he'd had assured her that with a bit of TLC, they would be gorgeous in years to come.

Lou wiped her face with her forearm, doing her best not to smear mud everywhere. Ha – who was she kidding? She must look a complete mess by this point... and frankly, she didn't care.

Bending low, she started to scoop together the last pile of trimmings. She'd just add these to the fire and then – as much as she hated the idea – she really needed to get ready for work. She took another deep breath and stared through the tangle of shoots and thorns ahead of her. There was still a lot to do – with any luck, Sean would agree to come back. Maybe next time she'd managed to muster the courage to ask him to join her for supper...

Wait – *what* was that?!

She'd just spotted something through the jumble of brambles in front of her.

'Hey – Sean?' she called, straightening up, still

peering in the direction of her discovery. Hmm, she couldn't see it from this height.

'You okay?' said Sean, appearing behind her in the patch she'd already cleared.

'I just spotted something through there,' she said, pointing.

'Where...? What kind of something?' he said, coming to stand next to her. 'You haven't unearthed one of those Shetland-pony-sized slugs you were on about, have you?'

Lou snorted and dug him in the ribs with her elbow.

'No!' she said, rolling her eyes. 'Hmm... I can't see it now I'm standing up.' She promptly squatted back down again, dragging him down with her.

Sean let out a groan, and Lou laughed. Clearly, he was feeling the effects of their day of solid gardening - thank heavens for that! Lou hadn't wanted to admit that she ached so much, she could no longer tell which bit of her it was coming from.

'There,' she said, pointing to the gleaming bit of... something... through the brambles. 'What do you reckon that is?'

'I see it!' said Sean. 'No idea... but I vote we take a hacking detour and find out before we finish for the day?'

Lou grinned at him and nodded. The pair of them let out identical groans as they struggled back to their feet.

'I think we're going to need a long bath tonight!' said Sean.

Lou smirked at him, and Sean's eyes grew wide. 'I mean... I didn't mean... not together... I mean... unless... erm...' he trailed off, his face turning a beautiful poppy red.

'Shall we find out what it is, then?' said Lou, deciding to let him straight off the hook. The poor bloke looked mortified - though the thought of sharing a bath with him really wasn't quite as bad as he was making it out to be!

'Yeah!' said Sean, turning gratefully to grab his hook.

As they hacked and slashed their way through the undergrowth towards Lou's discovery, she couldn't help but get more and more excited.

'It's a... is it a... shed?' she said.

'Looks like it!' said Sean with a nod, staring at the hint of faded yellow paintwork that was slowly coming into view.

It wasn't long before they'd hacked and trampled their way close enough to get a proper look.

'That's not a shed!' said Lou, her voice practically quivering with excitement.

'Nope!' said Sean, his eyes wide.

It was a beach hut. Right there in her garden. What was it doing up here so far away from the sea?! It looked like it had been lost in the undergrowth for years, judging by the mounds of brambles and thick swathes of weeds that had woven around it in a giant cocoon.

'It's quite big!' said Lou, staring at its gabled roof and double doors that were painted in a flaked and faded yellow. The rest of the wooden exterior was white – peeling slightly here and there but in remarkably good condition considering it had been lost in the mess of her back garden for so long.

Lou glanced at her watch again.

'I reckon I've just about got enough time for a quick look inside,' she said, 'if you've got time to give me a hand?'

'Are you kidding?' laughed Sean. 'I'm not going home now!'

Lou grinned at him.

It took some doing, but between the pair of them, they managed to clear the weeds from the front of the hut, making it easier for them to get to the doors. Then, with some difficulty, they shifted a couple of old, disintegrating concrete blocks out of the way.

'Well... go ahead!' said Sean, puffing slightly from the effort. 'It's your beach hut, after all!'

'I guess it is!' said Lou in wonder. It was a bit of an unlikely discovery, but a much nicer surprise than a giant pony-sized slug!

Lou wrapped her gloved fingers around the edge of one of the doors and did her best to ease it open. It wouldn't budge. She took a step back, readjusted her handhold and had another go. After a bit of a struggle, she managed to wiggle it open far enough to peep inside.

'No way!' she gasped, turning sparkling eyes towards Sean.

'What?' he said, staring back at her.

'Can you help me get it open a bit further?' she said.

Sean nodded and, stepping forwards, lifted the door gently until it swung over the rough ground.

'Wow!' he laughed, peering inside for the first time.

'I wasn't expecting there to be anything in there!' laughed Lou.

How wrong she was – the hut was packed with stuff. It seemed to echo with long-forgotten beach trips and laughter and ice cream. There were buckets and spades – though it had clearly been decades since they'd last been used to create a sandy fort. There were striped deckchairs and windbreaks rolled and stashed in the corners. A large, cracked plastic tub boasted an impressive collection of old inflatable armbands, and there was even a rubber ring with its very own – rather sad looking - dolphin head.

The hut was a treasure trove of mouldy, dusty, cobwebby wonders.

Lou couldn't stop a little wriggle from escaping, and she jostled Sean in her excitement, setting him laughing. Turning bright eyes to meet his, Lou caught her breath and suddenly stilled.

This man. This kind treasure of a human being. Without thinking about what she was doing, Lou leaned in closer and kissed him. Several long seconds passed until she pulled back – her eyes still fixed on his.

Sean looked surprised... but... delighted? She hoped she was reading this right.

'Well... that's the best reaction I've ever had to finding a mouldy old shed!' he said, his eyes twinkling.

Lou grinned, then shrugged and cleared her throat.

'Sorry,' she said.

Sean shook his head. 'Don't be... I think this goes down as my best afternoon ever.'

He reached out and ran an index finger gently down the side of her face, making Lou shiver slightly.

'Okay – it was a total lie anyway,' she said. 'I'm *not* sorry!'

It hadn't been an accident either. She had to face facts - she'd been dreaming about this moment ever since she'd watched him striding across North Beach in his swimming shorts. The real question was... did the reality live up to the dream?

Well... there was only one way to find out.

Lou reached out and laced her fingers through Sean's.

'I'm a bit out of practise!' she said, tugging him closer.

Sean promptly tripped over a hacked-down bramble sucker and crashed forwards. He wrapped his arms around her waist as he did his best to catch himself.

'Smooth!' he laughed as he straightened up. He was red in the face but his eyes were dancing with good-natured humour and delight. 'I was about to say "same"... but I think I just proved that without words!'

'I'll let you off!' said Lou, glad of any reason to have his strong arms wrapped around her, even if it was just to stop him from falling face-first into the undergrowth.

'May I?' said Sean, not taking his eyes off her.

Lou nodded. She wasn't really sure what he was asking, but frankly, whatever it was, she'd agree anyway.

Sean pulled her in even closer and Lou wound her arms around his neck as if she'd been doing it for years. It was strange how comfortable this felt. She was tall and had always dwarfed Brendan a bit. It had made her feel clumsy and oversized. But not Sean. He was tall and broad... and basically built like a Viking.

Right now, even covered in smears of mud and bits of rogue greenery, Lou felt sexy and confident – but also feminine and dainty in his arms.

Sean leaned in and kissed her again, and Lou promptly forgot to worry about anything. This was no accidental, hesitant kiss or quick peck. It was the kind of kiss that made her toes curl. It held the promise of what was to come... and it definitely didn't feel like he was out of practise!

'Okay,' said Sean, pulling back and looking a bit like he'd been hit over the head with a deckchair. 'It's official – the beach hut is the second favourite thing I've found in this garden today.'

'Knowing your thing for knackered old sheds, I'll take that as a huge compliment!' laughed Lou, snuggling into his side as if it was the most natural thing in the world. They stood staring at their discovery, Sean's arm draped easily over Lou's shoulders.

Lou was half expecting to spot a great big hole in the roof of the hut – or at least a bit that was sagging - but it looked like it had weathered its time in the undergrowth amazingly well. It definitely needed a bit of work if she was going to keep it though… but that was okay. Lou had a feeling she might know just the man for the job.

'Do you think… I mean…' she paused. Why did this feel more personal than snogging the poor guy's face off? 'Erm… would you be up for repairing it for me?' she said, finally managing to get the words out and flashing a shy glance at him.

'I thought you'd never ask!' said Sean with a huge smile, before dropping a kiss onto the top of her head.

CHAPTER 12

Lou had been floating ever since she'd finally said goodbye to Sean the previous day. It had been the most magical afternoon and she really hadn't wanted it to come to an end.

After their discovery, he'd helped her to clear all the way around the beach hut, and they'd chatted at full pelt – both of them aware their time was almost up.

It was the first time since getting her much-loved job at The Pebble Street Hotel that Lou had cursed her impending shift. Still, as she'd helped Sean to lift her dad's old lawnmower into the back of his truck - a job that kept being interrupted by a ridiculous amount of kissing – it became clear that it was probably a good thing he had to leave.

Lou had a feeling that if the evening had stretched out ahead of them, uninterrupted by annoying things like work, she'd have been sorely tempted to invite him to stay for supper… and maybe even a sleepover in her little bedroom under the eaves. As much as her entire body craved it – Lou didn't want to rush things.

It had been so many years since she'd experienced the sweet beginnings of something new, she'd forgotten how special those first kisses could be - the shy, tentative learning of each other and the intense anticipation of things to come. She didn't want to skip any of it!

Lou gave a little shiver of delight and sped up. She was on her way into town for her morning stint at The Sardine, and today she was actually glad that she had a busy day ahead of her. Today was a double-whammy – café this morning and hotel this afternoon and evening – but that was fine with her. A day off would have meant far too much time to drive herself to distraction re-living every moment of the previous day.

Of course, it would have been a different matter if there had been any chance of seeing Sean again today, but apparently, he was off on a mission to collect some old porthole windows from a shipyard on the other side of the country. If she was being honest, Lou was a bit gutted she wasn't going to get the chance to see him again for a few days… but perhaps it was for the best.

Sucking in a deep breath of sea air as she made her way down the hill towards the town, Lou stared out at the twinkling blue expanse. She knew she had the widest, goofiest smile on her face right now - and if anyone drove past and spotted her, it would probably be all over Seabury that she'd lost the plot.

Lou didn't care, though. She was truly, deeply happy – and not just because she'd kissed the most gorgeous man she'd ever laid eyes on! Yesterday had shown her that she wasn't broken. She wasn't permanently scarred by Brendan's betrayal. She'd just needed time to heal – and she had all the time in the world.

Of course, the fact that her very own beach hut had miraculously appeared out of the undergrowth was definitely the icing on the cake! Lou was keen to know more about it – especially as it was so full of treasures, but Sean hadn't had the faintest clue where it might have come from and why it was in her garden. He'd suggested she ask Charlie – and that was today's mission. Anything to distract her from the aches she had going on today – both from the weeding and the longing for more toe-curling kisses!

Lou picked up her pace until she was practically trotting along the seafront of West Beach towards The Sardine. The sea was so calm there was barely a wave, and there was just the merest shushing of the water as it played a backing track to the calls of the wheeling gulls.

This was probably Seabury at its finest, but frankly, Lou loved the little town whatever the weather – even when the waves were crashing right over the sea wall and the rain was driving sideways. She hoped she'd never forget how lucky she was to live here – surrounded by friends and new possibilities.

The Sardine appeared ahead of her, and Lou grinned at the sight. Kate had already set up the two little tables on the pavement and was no doubt getting the yard ready for their first al fresco customers of the day. Lou adored the café – it held so many good memories for her already... and now she had a feeling she'd never forget that first coffee she'd shared with Sean in there, either.

'Sentimental fool!' she muttered, just as Kate appeared in front of her.

'Did you say something?' said Kate, smiling at her.

Lou shook her head with a grin. 'Nope, just admiring the weather.'

'Hmm...' said Kate suspiciously, her eyes raking her from head to toe. 'If you say so.'

'I was!' laughed Lou.

'Well... it looks like you're enjoying very good "weather",' said Kate with a wink.

'I have no idea what you mean,' said Lou, feigning innocence as she headed into the café, with Kate following close behind her.

As much as she'd love to talk about Sean and everything that had happened yesterday – she couldn't. This was Seabury, and if she so much as breathed a hint of anything happening between them, it would be all over the town by lunchtime. By the time Sean got back from his trip, the gossips of Seabury would be unearthing their wedding hats and bulk-buying the confetti. And she *really* didn't want to scare him. Not this early in their... whatever this was!

'So?' said Kate curiously. 'What's put the wind in your sails today? Or should I say *who?!*'

'I found a beach hut in my back garden yesterday,' said Lou airily as she headed straight for the Italian Stallion to make herself a coffee.

'Wait... *what?!*' laughed Kate, staring at her with a look of bemusement. 'Of all the salacious bits of gossip I was hoping might come out of your mouth, that was probably the last thing I expected.'

Lou grinned at her as she set the machine gurgling. As the scent of strong, dark coffee rose to greet her, she had to work hard not to hug herself at the real reason for her blissed-out excitement.

'Yup!' she said. 'Right there in all those brambles in my back garden.'

'What was right there in the brambles?'

Ethel was struggling through the door, laden down with giant Tupperware boxes. It didn't seem like her full arms had prevented her bat-like hearing from picking up on the gossip, though. Lou quickly thanked her lucky stars that she hadn't decided to tell Kate about Sean yet!

'Apparently, Lou's found a beach hut in her back garden!' said Kate, rushing to hold the door open for Ethel.

'That's right,' said Ethel, nodding enthusiastically. 'I

heard you and Sean managed to uncover something while he was over with you yesterday!'

Lou's jaw dropped. How did this woman know everything? It was uncanny.

'Miss Lou... is that a blush?!' demanded Kate, peering at her.

Lou quickly shook her head and turned back to the coffee machine. 'Nope – just warm in here after the walk down, that's all!' she said over the whistling of the milk spout. She wasn't going to give in and tell these two troublemakers anything, no matter how much they bated her!

Luckily, Lou was saved by the bell... otherwise known as an unexpected early-morning rush. Lionel and Mary appeared for their breakfast date, closely followed by Doris from the post office - desperate for a takeaway coffee before she had to open the shop. Lou had just finished serving her when Mike and Sarah arrived with Stanley in tow... and then a bunch of tourists popped their heads in to ask if they could sit out in the yard.

Lou breathed a sigh of relief. She was well and truly off the hook. The ensuing chaos of getting everyone's orders ready, unpacking the fresh cakes Ethel had brought with her, and trying not to trip over Stanley as he decided to come and "help" her in the kitchen meant the risk of facing the inquisition had well and truly passed... for now.

Still, Lou went about her work with a smile plastered across her face. She couldn't help it. Yesterday had been blissful. The easy banter and laughter she'd shared with Sean had felt so natural. She really couldn't wait to see him again!

It didn't take Lou very long to get the mini-rush under control. She'd been at The Sardine long enough to know how to move around the cramped, cosy space without missing a beat.

'Ethel – would you mind hanging around for five minutes?' she said, as she waved Kate off on the day's sandwich round and began clearing the mess from the newly-vacated tables.

'Of course!' said Ethel with a wide smile. 'Oh – and don't forget there's a walnut cake in two halves in that bottom Tupperware – it still needs icing. It was still a bit too warm when I left home.'

'I can do that!' said Lou, quickly popping the top off the box so that the cake wouldn't sweat. She was greeted by a rush of warm, fresh cake that instantly made her mouth water.

'You know,' said Ethel, settling herself at her favourite table, 'I might just try one of those fancy hazelnut syrup coffees Doris is addicted to now it's gone quiet again.'

'Really?' said Lou, turning to look at her in surprise. Kate and Sarah had both been nagging Ethel to try one for ages.

'Yes... but don't go telling the other two that I caved!' she chuckled.

'Cross my heart!' said Lou, doing the motion and then crossing the tiny space to make Ethel's drink.

'And don't tell Charlie either!' said Ethel. 'That man's about as traditional as it gets.'

'I know!' laughed Lou. 'I offered him a pastry the other day.'

'I heard!' said Ethel. 'He was going on about it for days.'

Lou grinned. Charlie was dead set against pastries. He'd told her in no uncertain terms that he didn't believe in them – especially not when there was perfectly good cake on offer!

'Can I get you a croissant with this?' she asked Ethel lightly.

'Only if you promise never to tell him, and make sure I don't leave here with crumbs down my front!' said Ethel.

'You've got it!' said Lou, placing one on a plate along with a dish of fresh butter and a little bowl of strawberry jam.

She couldn't help but think all the subterfuge was hilarious – Charlie might be set in his ways when it came to his own preferences, but he adored Ethel and would do anything to make her happy.

'Thank you, dearie!' said Ethel as Lou placed everything down in front of her. 'Now... what was it you wanted to ask me?'

Lou watched Ethel piling jam onto her pastry and smiled. 'Well... it's about the beach hut. I was just wondering if you know anything about it? Like... why's it in my garden and who put it there!'

'Oh I know all about it,' said Ethel. 'I remember it well!'

'You do?!' said Lou excitedly, slipping into the chair opposite her friend. The tables out in the yard would just have to wait a moment for her to clear them.

'Absolutely, it's quite a sweet story, actually,' said Ethel pausing to take a tentative sip of coffee. 'It belonged to old Fred Hatch. He used to live in your place. He was a bit... eccentric? Anyway, the council decided to get rid of their beach huts. There used to be a lovely line of them along the sea wall over on North Beach – but in their wisdom, they decided they didn't want to pay for them to be removed every winter and put somewhere safe to stop them being blown away.'

'Blown away?' laughed Lou.

'Oh yes – it used to happen!' said Ethel seriously. 'So the council tried to sell them off, but old Fred was the only person who wanted one at the time. This was thirty years ago – or maybe more.'

'Okay...' said Lou. 'So Fred bought one and took it up to the cottage?'

'He bought one – but a specific one. Old Fred wanted the hut where he'd proposed to his late wife. The council delivered it and left it in the garden for him – but they got the wrong one. By the time he contacted them, the others had already been demolished and burned.' Ethel paused and let out a long sigh.

Lou clapped her hand to her mouth. 'Poor Fred!' she said. 'That must have been awful for him.'

'He wasn't happy, I can tell you that much!' said Ethel. 'Refused to pay for the hut and got into a long-running argument with the council that went on for years. It was a bit embarrassing for everyone, to be honest – especially as he was actually a member of the council himself!'

'Okay – this is starting to sound like a Seabury legend!' said Lou with a laugh.

'It is!' said Ethel, nodding fiercely. 'And it had consequences for the whole town.'

'How so?' said Lou.

'Well… they were good consequences, as it happens,' said Ethel. 'Fred decided to make life as difficult as he could for the council. He went on a one-man mission and made it practically impossible for them to get any business done. He voted against developers, against change, against planning. He always used to say - if you couldn't trust them to get a beach hut right, how could you trust them to do something like widen a road or build a new housing development without making mistakes that could destroy the town.'

'Well… he probably had a point,' said Lou with a shrug.

'Yep. I bet he did,' said Ethel. 'The man was a thorn in their side until he died… but in my opinion, he's a local hero and one of the main reasons Seabury is the way it is and not overrun with developments.'

Ethel paused and took another long sip of her coffee.

'Like it?' said Lou.

'Not bad – but I think I'll stick with my usual,' said Ethel. 'Now then – you're not planning on knocking that hut down or anything silly like that, are you? After all – that's a bit of Seabury's history you've unearthed there!'

'Don't worry about that,' said Lou, shaking her head. 'I'm going to get it repaired. Sean's going to fix it up for me'

'Sean, eh?' said Ethel, giving her a wry smile.

Lou could kick herself, she'd been doing so well at keeping him out of the conversation, and now she'd gone and dropped his name right back into proceedings!

'Erm... yeah,' she said.

'Well,' said Ethel, 'I can't wait to tell Charlie all about this. The hut, that is. Not Sean!' she winked at Lou.

Uh oh!

Why did Lou suddenly get the feeling she was about to star in her very own Seabury legend!

CHAPTER 13

Lou felt her heart do a double skip as Sean's truck pulled up outside the cottage. It might have been just a few days since their memorable discovery in her back garden, but it had felt like forever to her.

Lou had ached to see Sean again. She wanted to get to know him, spend time with him… and do some more kissing! In a way, she'd been glad that he'd gone on a trip. At least it had removed the temptation to loiter anywhere near Sandpiper Lane on the off chance she might bump into him!

The previous evening had been a nightmare, though. She knew he was back in town after his long drive from the other side of the country. Despite not wanting to bug him the moment he was home, it had taken every ounce of willpower she possessed not to swing past his house on her way home from work.

Lou really had done her best to lose herself in her shifts at the café and the hotel, and she'd even joined the Dippers for a quick swim the previous morning. It hadn't really helped matters, though. Logically, she'd known Sean wouldn't be on the beach, but that hadn't stopped her eyes from scanning the pebbles for him… just in case she'd got the days mixed up.

Despite her promise to herself not to let the cat out of the bag just yet, she'd ached to talk to someone about him. Having to stay quiet was making the mad craving to see him worse. Even so, she was determined to keep their kissing session to herself. She didn't want to tell Kate, Hattie or any of her other Seabury friends until she knew whether it was going to be a one-off thing… or something more interesting.

Urgh – just the thought of that wonderful day out in the garden together being a one-off made Lou feel itchy all over. She'd tossed and turned in bed the night before, her dreams full of Sean's soft lips and the promise of lazy walks on the beach together before coming home and exploring every inch of each other…

The idea that might not happen - that she might have got the wrong end of the stick - made her feel slightly sick. Or maybe that was just the sheer bolt of lust that was running through her at the sight of him again!

'Hi!' he said, hopping out of the driver's seat and grinning at her across the back of his truck.

'Hey!' she said with a slow smile.

What was this man doing to her?

Lou shivered as her spine tingled. Surely their kisses in the garden couldn't be a one-off? That would be a total waste of the most insane chemistry she'd ever felt.

'I've got a surprise for you,' said Sean, his smile getting even wider.

'Oh?' said Lou, giving her head a little shake and doing her best to drag herself out from the drift of imaginary pink hearts and confetti that seemed to be swirling in the air around them.

Sean reached into the back of the truck and indicated for her to come closer before whisking a tarp away.

'Oh my goodness!' she gasped. It was her dad's old lawnmower. Sean had beaten most of the dents out of it and had given it a coat of beautiful, glossy paint. It looked practically brand new. 'I can't believe it!'

'All repaired and ready to go,' said Sean, leaning in to give it a pat. 'She's such a lovely old thing and she deserved some TLC.'

'Thank you. So much!' said Lou, her voice feeling thick in her throat. She couldn't help it. Now the old lawnmower would just remind her of her old dad, rather than all the abuse Brendan had thrown at it over the years. 'How on earth did you find the time?!'

'It's no problem!' said Sean. 'And it stopped me from coming over and bugging you the minute I got home yesterday!' he added with a sheepish smile.

Lou did her best to hide her own smile. It sounded like they'd both had very similar evenings! She quickly reached into the back of the truck to help Sean lift the mower down to safety – and nearly ended up dropping her side when jolts of electricity dashed across her skin as his arm brushed hers.

Get a grip woman!

She needed to get control of herself, otherwise she was going to end up jumping on the poor guy right here in front of the cottage.

'Right,' said Sean, 'that's that done. And I've got news... but first...'

He reached out and took Lou's hand, swinging her into him and pulling her in for a long, soft kiss. Lou felt her toes curl. Okay – so she definitely hadn't got the wrong end of the stick, then! By the time Sean pulled away, she was out of breath and grinning from ear to ear.

'What?!' he laughed, taking in her expression.

'Just glad I didn't dream what happened between us in front of the beach hut, that's all!' she said.

'You didn't,' said Sean, 'though if we're talking dreams here, you've definitely starred in a few of mine!'

Lou felt her cheeks heat up. Oh blimey – at this rate, they weren't going to manage to get any gardening done today!

'Okay...' she gulped. 'And... erm... are you going to tell me what I was getting up to in those dreams?'

Sean shook his head. 'No way. That's more third-date territory!'

'I'll just have to be patient then!' said Lou.

'Good at that, are you?' said Sean with a naughty wink.

'Not on your life!' chuckled Lou. 'Sure I can't persuade you?'

'Tempting... but right now I've got something to tell you!' said Sean, taking charge of the old mower and trundling it towards the garage. She yanked open the rickety old wooden door for him and watched as he pushed the mower inside, tucking it up tenderly under its tarpaulin.

'And?!' said Lou, on tenterhooks but not wanting to push him – especially as he straightened up and instantly wrapped an arm around her waist, making her brain go all fluffy.

'Well,' said Sean, giving her a peck on the cheek and practically making her swoon in the process, 'word has spread quickly around the allotments-'

'Oh god!' sighed Lou, instantly jumping in. 'I'm so sorry! I have no idea how that happened – I swear I didn't tell anyone about us and-'

'Woah!' laughed Sean. 'Don't panic – our not-so-dirty little secret isn't out yet.'

'Oh,' said Lou, pulling up short. 'Oh... so what...'

'We'll come back to why that's an issue in a minute,' chuckled Sean.

'Not an issue... just Seabury...' muttered Lou.

'Don't worry – I'm just teasing. I know what it's like around here,' said Sean with a wry smile. 'You can't sneeze without the entire town buying you boxes of tissues!'

Lou laughed, feeling her shoulders drop in relief.

'Don't know why you're laughing,' Sean said. 'True story!'

'I don't doubt it!' said Lou. 'So... erm, what news is spreading fast?'

'About the hut!' said Sean, grabbing her hand and leading her around to the back garden. 'Seems Fred Hatch is a bit of a hero up there.'

'How do you know about that?' said Lou, mildly bemused.

'Ethel told Charlie, Charlie told Ben, Ben told me when he was helping me load your mower this morning.'

'Is nothing sacred?' said Lou, stopping to admire the space they'd managed to clear a few days ago. They'd managed to get a lot done... but they'd probably be at it for weeks before they managed to reach the boundaries of her garden!

'Of course nothing's sacred,' said Sean. 'This is Seabury!'

'Very good point!' said Lou. 'Anyway – you said there was news?'

'I was getting to that bit!' said Sean. 'And yes – I can see patience *isn't* a strong point.'

'Oi!' said Lou, digging him in the ribs. He promptly

retaliated by ruffling her hair.

'I hear Ethel told you all about Fred's single-handed efforts to cause as much havoc for the council as possible?' he said.

Lou nodded.

'Well – everyone remembers him as a grumpy old soul – but it sounds like he had a really good heart and they all loved him,' said Sean. 'Now they know you've rediscovered his beach hut - and that you're clearing the garden – so they all want to help if they can.'

'They do?!' said Lou in surprise.

Sean nodded. 'I was thinking... maybe if everyone turns up on the same day, we could get the rest of it cleared in a matter of hours instead of weeks!'

'Wow!' said Lou. It was almost as if he'd read her mind and picked up on what she'd been thinking just a few seconds ago.

'I mean – it's totally up to you, of course!' said Sean quickly, clearly taking her surprise as hesitation. 'I didn't want to say yes or no one way or another as it's not my house and it wasn't my place until I'd spoken to you... but they're definitely waiting for me to report back!' He paused. 'So... what do you think?'

'I think it's amazing!' said Lou, her eyes wide.

She knew the main reason they all wanted to help out was to honour the memory of Fred... but still, she was incredibly touched. The fact that they were all willing to give up their time to help her out meant more than she could express. Some days, Seabury was almost overwhelming when it came to the amount of love and friendship that seemed to flow in the community. Sure, it had its occasional downsides – like the finely-tuned jungle drums – but the upsides always won the contest.

'How many people are we talking, here?' she said. She'd barely had anyone over to the cottage yet. It was in such a state and she still had so much left to do – not to mention that the place was barely big enough for one person, let alone an onslaught of guests!

Sean stared at the hut, obviously doing some sums in his head. 'Maybe... something like thirty?' he said.

'*What?!*' gasped Lou. 'I mean – that's amazing and everything... but how would I even make them all cups of tea? I don't even have that many cups for starters... and they'll all need something to eat too. Wow... this could get out of hand really fast!'

Suddenly, Lou wanted to duck out of the whole thing and go back to struggling along on her own. Sure, it would take her forever to get the job done, but at least she wouldn't end up letting everyone down after they'd all been kind enough to volunteer to help her out!

'Maybe... maybe I could just boil the kettle constantly and wash the cups up on some sort of rota... *what?!*' she demanded, suddenly noticing that Sean was watching her with a smile on his face. He was gently shaking his head as if the whole thing was funny.

'You!' he said. 'You always think of others first. I've

noticed this about you... probably before you even knew I existed. You'll do anything for anyone. All these people want to come and help you, and you instantly start worrying about their comfort.'

'Oh,' said Lou in surprise. Yet again, Sean had her on the hop. And what did he mean "before she even knew he existed"?! She'd have to figure that one out later. 'Well... thanks, I think?' she said.

Sean shrugged. 'It's another reason I like you so much, that's all.'

Lou instantly started wondering what the other reason might be... this man was far too distracting to have around when there were serious issues to deal with... like the fact half of Seabury's allotment holders were going to descend on her tiny cottage and overgrown back garden.

'So... you like the idea?' prompted Sean.

Lou nodded. 'I'll just have to figure out the logistics, I guess.'

'Nah,' said Sean. 'You don't need to worry about that. Kate and Hattie have already both volunteered to feed the crowd if you agree to do it. Free of charge, of course!'

'Wait... what?' laughed Lou. 'Haven't you been away? How on earth have you been arranging all this? And how come no one thought to mention it to me?'

'Ah... the modern invention of mobile phones!' laughed Sean. 'And sorry I didn't run it past you first – I wanted to talk to you face to face about the whole thing. Both Kate and Hattie were under strict instructions not to mention a word until I'd checked you were up for it... I mean, it's a lot of people to have descend on your house!'

'But... I don't get how this is all happening so fast?!' she said with a slightly hysterical giggle.

'You don't mind, do you?' said Sean, looking a bit worried. 'I mean, it's really not a problem if you don't want to do it. They all just got so excited about the idea – I was fielding texts all day! But I don't want you to feel obliged to let it happen. I'd hate it if you felt forced into letting a bunch of randoms invade your back garden!'

'No – I love it,' said Lou quickly. 'Really! she added when he continued to frown in concern. 'It'll be a wonderful way to get it all done. The more the merrier! And it just goes to show how popular old Fred really was, doesn't it?!'

'No Lou,' said Sean, reaching out and squeezing her hand. 'It goes to show how popular *you* are. Everyone adores you.'

'I... I'm not sure I deserve that,' she said quietly.

'You don't have to *deserve* being liked and loved, you know?' said Sean. 'It's not some kind of barter system where you have to give to get. No one's keeping tally!'

Lou looked at him in surprise.

It wasn't? *It wasn't!*

Suddenly, some kind of strange, cosmic penny dropped. She could just be herself... and that was enough? She didn't have to apologise, or ask permission just to take up space?

'Okay,' she said, blinking hard.

'Okay?' said Sean, turning to her, his eyebrows raised.

Lou wondered briefly if he had any idea what had just happened in her head... and the fact that he'd just helped her to clear almost two decades worth of baggage in about twenty seconds.

'Okay,' she whispered again, leaning forward and kissing him gently.

'You know,' said Sean when they finally broke apart, 'I had some ideas about sorting out the beach hut for you while I was away.'

Lou wriggled with excitement. 'Tell me!'

'Well... I was wondering... would you trust me to just do them for you as a surprise?' he asked.

Lou stared at him for a long moment. Then, thinking of the magical spaces he'd created in his own back garden, she nodded in excitement.

'I trust you,' she said.

'And you're okay with not sneaking a peek until I'm finished?' he said, raising an eyebrow and giving her a knowing look.

Lou bit her lip. Maybe this would be one of those rare times she'd actually managed to dig up a bit of patience from somewhere.

'Okay, fine,' she said, giving a theatrical sigh, before grabbing him for another kiss.

CHAPTER 14

Someone had made a sign and strung it up on Lou's gate.

"Gardening Party here today!"

There was an impressive drawing of a sleeping dragon wound around the words. Lou was firmly intending to steal the sign when the party was over so that she could frame it and hang it in the living room. In the meantime, she could only cross her fingers that none of them uncovered an actual dragon in the undergrowth today... the beach hut had been enough of a surprise.

As much as she loved the sign, it didn't really seem to be necessary. It looked like everyone in Seabury knew where to find her, and way more people had turned up than she'd been expecting. The thing that had surprised her most was that she knew almost all of them by name or - at the very least - by sight.

Clearly working at both Pebble Street and The Sardine had paid off. Lou got to see a lot of the locals nearly on a daily basis, and she'd become a part of this wonderful, caring - slightly nutty - community almost by accident.

All the allotment holders had turned up, as well as most of the Chilly Dippers too. It was a peculiar mixture – but it seemed to be working out well so far if the piles of decimated weeds and newly-cleared garden were anything to go by.

Lou was touched that all her friends had rocked up to help – otherwise she really would have been boiling the kettle on repeat and washing mugs all day! Hattie and Kate had appeared with enough food to feed an army, and thankfully, Mike had brought a big hot water urn from New York Froth, as well as two massive crates of spare mugs and plates.

'Sweet treat?' said Sarah, coming up to her bearing a large Tupperware box.

'One of your concoctions?' said Lou, staring down at the immaculately iced cupcakes in their canary-yellow cases.

'Of course!' laughed Sarah. 'The trick is… can you guess my secret ingredient?'

Lou had been about to pluck one out of the box, but she hesitated for a second. Sarah's experimental phase had been going on for a few months now. The cakes invariably tasted like heaven... but there had been a couple of times she'd wanted to spit them back out as soon as the intrepid baker had revealed her secret ingredient.

'What flavour are they?' asked Lou, suspiciously.

'Yeah right!' laughed Sarah. 'I'm not spoiling the game that easily. No one's managed to guess it yet though!'

Lou stared at her.

'It's fine... it's nothing gross,' said Sarah, rolling her eyes. 'They're in honour of it being a gardening party.'

Lou bent low over the cakes and stared hard at them. They looked pretty innocent – but knowing Sarah they were probably grass-fermented or something equally as nuts.

'Give me the best comparison, then,' said Lou.

'What do you mean?' said Sarah frowning.

'You know – "If you like lemon drizzle cake, you'll love these." She said, determined not to be caught out.

'Ooh, good idea,' said Sarah. 'Okay – if you love carrot cake... and the colour red - then you'll love these.'

Look giggled and shook her head, none the wiser. 'Okay. I do love carrot cake,' she said, reaching in and taking one.

'No nibbling,' said Sarah, watching her closely. 'I want to see cake and icing going in!'

'Yes boss!' said Lou, before mentally crossing her fingers and taking a bite.

She let out a long, low groan of delight before quickly checking around her to make sure no one had overheard her make such a filthy sound in public.

'You know,' said Sarah, 'I'm going to have to start recording your cake reaction sounds. You'd go viral online in seconds!'

Lou shook her head in horror, though her mouth was too full of cake and icing to say anything.

'Spoilsport!' said Sarah. 'Anyway – any guesses?'

Lou cocked her head. The cake was sweet and moist, but there was a tangy depth of flavour to it that made her think of treacle... or molasses...

'I give up!' she said, with a shrug.

'Tomato soup,' whispered a beaming Sarah.

'Very funny,' said Lou.

'Really. It's tomato soup.'

Lou wrinkled her nose and hesitated for a moment before taking another bite. The cake was too delicious not to just double-check.

'You know – I'm really going to miss your crazy taste sensations when you start your apprenticeship!' she said through a mouthful of icing, staring at the kid in front of her who'd grown up way too fast. Sarah seemed to have turned from a child into a gorgeous young woman practically overnight.

'Don't!' sighed Sarah. 'Kate's already stocking up on the Kleenex ready for when I move out. She reckons she's going to cry for at least a month.'

'What about your dad?' said Lou, glancing over to where Mike was helping Kate with the food.

'I think he's just pretending it's not happening,' said Sarah. 'It's easier to deal with, to be honest. Anyway – you're stuck with me all summer yet, so don't go blubbing on my cupcakes!'

'Fair enough!' grinned Lou. 'Now... do me a favour and go surprise Sean with these, will you? I want to see his face when you tell him what's in them!'

'You've got it!' said Sarah, giving Lou a huge wink and making a beeline straight for Sean, who was carefully strimming around the beach hut.

The hut was Sean's territory now – and Lou had stuck faithfully to her promise not to peek inside until he'd finished whatever he was up to. She'd helped him to stash all the dusty, beachy treasures in the back of her garage, and that was it – her last glimpse of the thing until he'd worked his magic on it.

Lou had discovered that it was easy to be patient when the project meant that Sean visited the cottage most days. She didn't want to think too much about what would happen after he'd finished... but so far, the signs were looking promising!

She watched as Sarah plied him with the cupcakes and then let out a hoot of laughter when he turned to stare at her across the garden – mid-bite. It looked like the young baker had dropped her in it at the same time as revealing the secret ingredient. She gave him a flirty wave, and Sean shook his head slowly as a smile lit up his face. Lou's insides melted. Even at a distance with a tomato soup cupcake in hand, Sean had the power to turn her to mush.

Lou quickly turned away – it wouldn't do to get all hot and bothered while she had a garden full of guests! She peered around, shaking her head in amazement at the small army of friends who'd turned up to help her conquer the jungle. She'd made sure to pull her weight too, and they had all worked together - hacking, raking, piling and generally working their way outwards as they hunted for the boundaries of the garden. A huge cheer had gone up when Ben had finally managed to reveal one of the old stone walls.

It really had been a brilliant day so far, and Lou had even enjoyed Jean's constant attempts to talk her into growing some broad beans. She'd laughed along with everyone else when Cyril Nolan had tried to convince her that her best bet would be to cover the entire garden with old carpet offcuts and just leave it for a couple of years. Lou had to hand it to him, the guy was pretty persistent, and she had several discount vouchers for his family business tucked away in her jeans pockets.

Lou hadn't really had much chance to speak to Sean – there had simply been so much to do and too many people to talk to. They seemed to have been working at opposite ends of the garden most of the morning – but somehow, it just didn't matter. Whenever she caught his eye, he smiled at her – instantly melting her insides and causing her to lose the power of speech. They'd shared little waves too - making her feel like a teenager with the biggest crush ever, every shared moment making her day... week... maybe even month.

By lunchtime – amazingly – it was all done. The boundaries had been discovered, no one had tumbled over the edge of the cliff, and everyone was excitedly heading for the folding tables where Mike, Kate and Hattie had been busy laying out a feast. There were cakes galore from The Sardine, gourmet sandwiches from Pebble Street, and gallons of tea, coffee and cold drinks courtesy of New York Froth. There were even platters of fruit and veggies from the allotments, along with bowls of delicious-looking dips.

It was organised chaos, and Lou kept having to swallow down waves of emotion that all these wonderful people had turned up to help her. She just couldn't get over it.

As she joined the long line of people patiently waiting to wash their hands at her tiny kitchen basin, Lou's attention fell on another, slightly smaller group of people gathered around someone sitting on an old wooden stool.

'What's going on over there?' she asked the woman in front of her.

Until today, Lou had only known her as "earl grey tea with a squeeze of lemon", but now she knew her name was Kathleen – one of the allotment holders who liked to grow edible flowers on her patch.

'Oh – that's the line for first aid!' said Kathleen. 'Lovely Ben's over there pulling out prickles and sticking plasters on scrapes.'

'What a hero!' laughed Lou.

'I know – though I had to move away from that lot just now because everyone's having far too much fun discussing all the disgusting accidents they've had in the garden.'

'Nice!' said Lou. 'Just before lunch too!'

'Yeah... I didn't much fancy any more "fork through my foot" brags!' she laughed.

'Eew!' said Lou.

'By the way – thank you for inviting me, I've had the best time,' said Kathleen.

Lou stared at her for a moment. 'Are you joking? Thank you for coming and attacking my jungle.'

'I always wanted to say hi and see if you fancied hanging out sometime...' She paused and dug her toe into the ground. 'Sorry – I sound like a primary school kid!'

'No you don't!' said Lou. 'And I'd love to!'

'Really?' said Kathleen, her face lighting up. 'You're always so busy, and in the thick of things and... well... popular.'

Lou laughed and shook her head. 'Humans are a weird bunch, aren't we?! You think that – but I'm a total mess.'

'I think we all are in our own way,' said Kathleen with a smile.

'Amen to that!' said Lou. 'Anyway, I'd love to hang out! I need all the friends I can get.'

Kathleen grinned at her and then nodded at Lou's newly re-discovered garden and the dozens of chatting, happy people. 'Well – in that case... I'd say you're doing okay on that score.'

'I actually can't believe it,' said Lou, her voice low. 'Thank heavens for Seabury.'

'Well – yes,' said Kathleen slowly. 'But it's you too, you know. People are drawn to kindness.'

Lou opened her mouth to reply, but no sound came out. Kathleen just smiled, patted her on the arm, and then disappeared into the kitchen to take her turn at the sink.

CHAPTER 15

'Croissant and a flat white for you Cyril, and carrot cake and a pot of tea for you Frank?' said Lou, popping the tray down in front of the two gents sitting at a sunlit table in The Sardine's courtyard.

'Perfect – thanks Lou!' said Cyril.

'We were just wondering – are you planning on hosting any more gardening parties?' said Frank, looking up at her with an eager expression on his face.

'Oh!' said Lou in surprise. 'Well... to be honest, I haven't quite got over the last one... but maybe!'

'Well let us know if you do,' said Cyril. 'We'd all be more than happy to pitch in again.'

'Absolutely,' nodded Frank. 'Highlight of the year so far, I'd say!'

Lou smiled at them and promised they'd be the first to know if she decided to do it again. In the two weeks since the gardening party, Lou had been fielding questions like this almost daily. The party was the talk of the town, and the fact that everyone seemed to have had such a good time was a source of real joy – even though Lou could hardly take any credit for its success. The whole thing seemed to have organised itself around her.

Speaking of fielding questions, the gardening party wasn't the only hot topic in town. Seabury's entire population seemed to be invested in how Sean was getting on with the restoration of the old beach hut. Of course, Lou couldn't tell them anything. Sean was working like a ninja – disappearing inside for long hours and not breathing a word to her about what he was up to.

Lou hadn't even peeped under the giant tarpaulin that he'd pulled over the whole thing to "keep the seagull poop off." All she knew was that he'd had a few things delivered directly to the cottage – but as they'd arrived while she'd been at work, she hadn't even managed to catch a glimpse of these intriguing packages.

As much as she was having fun teasing Sean about how long he was taking, she was secretly loving the anticipation. It took a serious amount of willpower not to take a sneaky peek whenever he went home… but there was no way she was willing to spoil the surprise now.

'Right,' said Lou as she bounded back into the café,

making Kate jump, 'that's me done for the day unless you need a hand with anything else?'

Kate shook her head with a grin. 'No – you carry on. Isn't today the big reveal?'

Lou nodded, unwrapping her apron as fast as her fingers would let her. 'Yep. He's been at it for ages.'

'And you really haven't got a clue what he's done to it?' said Kate.

'Nope,' said Lou, shaking her head. 'But… well, you've seen what he does, right?'

'Oh yes!' laughed Kate. 'I know what I'll be getting for Mike for his birthday. We've got all that space in the lighthouse, but the minute he saw those cosy little caves in Sean's back garden, he wanted one.'

'Yeah… I know how he feels,' sighed Lou.

'About the sheds… or about the man building them?' said Kate, raising her eyebrows.

'Oh hush,' muttered Lou.

'What's going on with you two?' said Kate curiously. 'You could hardly keep your eyes off each other at the gardening party. I swear I got burned when I was standing between the pair of you.'

'Nothing to report!' said Lou, in a singsong voice.

As much as she wanted to tell both Kate and Hattie how she was feeling, there was something rather lovely about keeping this thing with Sean just for the pair of them…just for now. Lou knew that people would find out eventually… but right now, the stolen kisses and cuddles in her garden, and the long evenings drinking wine together curled up in her tiny cottage were precious.

'*Nothing?*' demanded Kate. 'Yeah right. Every time someone says his name, you light up. You're not telling me you haven't had your wicked way with him?'

'That's exactly what I'm telling you,' said Lou, giving her friend a pious look before turning her back and grinning at the wall as she slipped her coat on. Well... it was true... kind of. She *hadn't*... not yet at least.

'Well... *I* believe you but thousands wouldn't,' said Kate.

'I'll see you tomorrow?' said Lou.

'You're on Trixie in the morning – if you're still up for it?' said Kate hopefully.

'Always,' said Lou.

~

It was as much as Lou could do not to break into a trot on her way back up the hill towards her cottage. She was exhausted – but it didn't matter. She had a couple of hours off before she was due for her shift at Pebble Street, and she didn't want to waste a single second of it. Sean was at the cottage working on the beach hut and he'd mentioned that today might be the day for the big reveal.

Lou hadn't been lying when she'd told Kate that nothing had happened between the pair of them yet... but for some reason, today held the promise of something more. Sure, they'd spent tons of time together when he emerged, blinking from under the tarp with sawdust in his hair. There had been several lovely, long evenings discussing what she wanted to do with the garden and marking out the space with bits of string.

Nothing seemed to make Sean happier than helping her to figure out exactly what she wanted from the garden. The fact that he was an absolute genius when it came to plant names definitely helped matters!

Lou had been embarrassed at first when she'd started trying to describe the bright red flowers and glossy leaves of the shrub she'd always wanted to grow – but he'd listened carefully and then pulled up a photo of a Camellia on his phone. Lou had let out a cheer – and it had promptly become one of their favourite games.

Sean was never pushy – he just offered gentle advice whenever she asked for it. He hadn't laughed at her when she'd told him that she wanted to mix veggies and flowers in the same beds, and on his next visit he'd handed her a book on companion planting.

Every single conversation she had with him made Lou fall a tiny bit further in ... *whatever*. She was not going to use the L word! Sean was amazing – and she loved spending time with him. That was all.

Lou was panting by the time she reached her little front garden gate, but she didn't pause for breath. She hurried straight around to the back garden, only to find Sean sitting on one of the old, striped deck chairs with his feet up.

'Ah ha!' she said with a laugh. 'Skiving, I see!'

Sean leapt to his feet, bounded towards her and wrapped her in a hug.

'I'm all hot and sweaty!' she laughed, trying to pull away.

'And I don't care!' chuckled Sean, kissing her neck and making her squirm. 'And I'm skiving because... I've finished!'

'You *have*?!' she squeaked. He might have hinted that today would be the big reveal, but she'd not fully let herself believe it. Years and years of being let down, of waiting only to be disappointed over and over again always rose up to spoil the giddy anticipation.

'Why the tone of surprise?' he laughed, raising his eyebrows.

'History,' she sighed, 'ancient history.'

'Want to talk about it?' said Sean.

Lou looked at him, cocking her head as she thought about it. She could see from his face that the offer was genuine. He'd listen for as long as she needed to rant. He'd hear her out without telling her that she was wrong, or that she should feel something different. But suddenly – she didn't want to talk about Brendan. He just wasn't worth it. She was finally ready to drop him from her life – just like he'd dropped her from his.

'You know what,' said Lou, 'no thanks. It's not important – not anymore.'

'Cool,' said Sean, simply. 'So – are you ready for your surprise?'

Lou shivered with excitement, her toes curling inside her trainers. 'I've been ready since the day I met you, I think.'

'Erm... we *are* just talking about the beach hut here, right?' laughed Sean.

Lou wiggled her eyebrows. 'Depends on what kind of job you've done!'

She watched as Sean's eyes grew wide with delight. 'Well... fingers crossed you like it then! Grab the tarp!'

'You've got it!' said Lou, rushing across the uneven ground and grabbing a corner, ready to fling it aside like she'd been dying to for the last two weeks.

Lou turned, waiting for him to take the other corner, but he just stood there. She was surprised to see a nervous look flash across his face. It wasn't something she'd ever seen on him before.

'You want to help?' she said with a smile.

'It's your hut,' Sean shrugged. 'I thought you'd want the honours!'

Lou shook her head. 'Together,' she said. 'Grab the other corner.'

Sean grinned at her, hurried forwards and took a handful of the rough green plastic.

'Three!' said Lou. 'Two...'

'One!' they chorused, and with a yank, the tarp fluttered clear of the old beach hut.

Lou took a deep breath, staring at what they'd just

uncovered. It was still unmistakably the beach hut the pair of them had discovered in the undergrowth several weeks ago. She'd half-dreaded the idea that it might have been totally transformed – but this was perfect. It had simply been restored to its former glory.

'The real changes are on the inside,' said Sean quietly.

Lou nodded, not wanting to say anything. She stepped forwards and with trembling fingers, reached out to open the door. It swung open easily, revealing a beautifully light, airy space.

'Okay, wow!' she breathed, staring around.

There was a new roof light which was bathing the hut in sunshine. A tiny wood burner sat in the corner on a slate hearth, its chimney stretching up and out through the ceiling. How on earth had she missed that from the outside?!

'How did you sneak a fire in here?!' she gasped.

'Magic!' chuckled Sean, following her inside.

'This is unreal,' said Lou, her voice unsteady as she stared at the comfy-looking sofa and a bookcase piled high with gardening magazines. A new window on the opposite side of the hut boasted a wooden sill complete with a row of small plants in pots.

'There's this too,' said Sean, edging around her to unfold a small, wire-framed chair with a wooden seat.

'Why would you sit on that when you've got a sofa?' said Lou with a huge smile as she flopped down onto its primrose cushions.

'Well,' said Sean, fiddling with a wooden catch, 'I thought it might come in handy if you wanted to sit at this.'

With a flourish, he drew out a small but perfectly formed desk which had been masquerading as a wall panel. Lou's mouth dropped open. For once in her life, she found herself completely speechless. He'd done all this... for her?

'I'm really sorry about the step up into the hut,' he said, 'but I had to do something to insulate the floor otherwise there was no way the space would hold any warmth! I've insulated the walls too – I would have liked to use something a bit thicker, but it's already quite small in here and I didn't want you losing any more room than you had to.'

'You're seriously apologising to me right now?' laughed Lou.

Sean shrugged. 'I get caught up in the details,' he said with a sheepish grin.

'It shows,' she said, staring around her incredulously. 'In the best way. Tell me more!'

'Well,' said Sean, ruffling his hair in a way that made Lou want to kiss his face off, 'the wood burner is all tested and good to go... and if you don't like the plants we can swap them for something else – but Eddie up at the allotments thought you might like these little succulents to start with.'

'I cannot believe you snuck a sofa in here without me noticing,' said Lou, shaking her head.

'Ah well, you can thank Lionel for the sofa... and the desk chair,' he said with a smile. 'They're not new – obviously – but there's life in them yet. They were the perfect size, and he says he hopes you like them!'

'Like them?' said Lou, the words coming out in a muffled kind of sob. She was suddenly as close to tears as it was possible to get without a torrent of them cascading down her face. 'Thank you, I love them.'

Great! Now, she was crying properly!

Frantically trying to mop her ridiculous tears away, Lou registered a warm weight landing next to her as Sean joined her on the sofa. A split second later, he wrapped his arms around her. She burrowed against his chest, letting her tears soak into the front of his shirt as she vowed never, ever to let go of this wonderful man. They'd simply have to stay cocooned together on this sofa forever.

CHAPTER 16

It was a beautiful day. Lou gleefully wriggled her toes into the sun-warmed sand of West Beach, thanking her lucky stars that the Chilly Dippers had opted for a sandy beach swim today instead of heading over to the pebbles of North Beach.

She stared dreamily out to sea as Stanley's tail gently paffed her on the back as he wagged in excitement. He was clearly looking forward to his swim. It was Sean's fault he was here, of course. These days, Stanley much preferred swimming with Sean than the Dippers. They'd swim for miles together, and that meant there was much more chance he'd get to meet up with his seal friends. But today, Sean was swimming with Lou and the Chilly Dippers, so Stanley was there too.

'Good lad,' said Lou, rubbing the big bear's head. She'd promised Kate they'd take him back to The

Sardine when they were finished, so she felt responsible for keeping an eye on their furry gooseberry... she could really do without him heading off after a piece of driftwood or passing seal. As long as he didn't slobber all over her towel...

'Too late!' she sighed, turning to see that he was doing just that. She grinned as he stretched out behind her, making a furry bolster cushion across her back.

The ranks of the Chilly Dippers had increased substantially over the last couple of weeks. The lovely weather had brought a few of the older members out of retirement – but there were plenty of newbies in the group too. Lou had invited Kathleen to join her at their last swim, and her new friend had taken to it like a duck... to a brick wall. There had been a lot of shrieking and giggling the minute the water reached her knees – but considering that was the case for most of the Dippers, she was welcomed with open arms!

Lou watched the little gaggle of women as they started to drop their towels and pull on swim-caps ready to take the plunge. It was all so familiar to her now – friendly and fun. Of course, the allotment crowd and the Dippers knew each other individually, but until the gardening party, they'd never had the chance to mix before. Today – after Kathleen's glowing report - there was a good number of intrepid allotment holders ready for their first time out with the Dippers. Even Jean was there – having deserted her beloved broad beans for a few hours.

Lou's eyes landed on Sean as he stood in the sunshine, looking as glorious as ever in his swim shorts. He was busy chatting with the slightly chilly-looking gardeners, and Lou wondered if Cyril was trying to take his mind off the impending swim by extolling the virtues of carpet to them all. Whatever they were talking about, Sean had his usual massive smile plastered on his face.

Lou sighed and stroked Stanley. 'We like him a lot, don't we boy?'

Stanley just opened his mouth and grinned at her as he started to pant.

'Yeah – I know,' she laughed. 'Ooof!'

The big dog had just jumped to his feet, sending Lou face-first into the sand. With an excited bark, Stanley took off and headed for the sea at a gallop. Lou struggled to her feet ready to give chase, only to see that he was racing Jean, who was hurtling down the beach away from the gardeners and towards the waves.

A huge cheer went up as Jean took a running dive straight into the sea with Stanley hot on her heels. Clearly, he'd had enough of waiting for Sean and Lou to get on with it and had chosen a new swim buddy for the day.

Lou's eyes drifted back to Sean again. He was cheering with everyone else, his hands over his head as he applauded Jean's bravery. She felt her heart throb as she watched him.

Lou knew she had a big, goofy smile on her face

again, but she didn't care - she was way past pretending there wasn't anything happening between them. That had come to an abrupt end after Sean had insisted that the beach hut needed christening properly. They'd shared a particularly memorable sleepover on the primrose-covered sofa.

Bursting with excitement and surrounded with her imaginary swirl of hearts and confetti again, Lou had promptly organised a very memorable – and raucous - evening of pure girly gossip with Kathleen, Kate and Hattie. They'd all joined her at the cottage along with a case of Upper Bamton's finest rose that Lionel donated to the cause.

And so – Lou had spilt the beans in style – delighting her friends with the tale of just how much she liked the big-hearted man she'd met through an underwater headbutt! It could have turned out so differently – but Lou was so happy that it hadn't.

Suddenly, life was full of fun and sunshine, and Lou was almost overwhelmed with happiness to be exploring it with a man who was as kind as he was gorgeous - a man who seemed to want nothing more than to make her happy. Sure... his obsession with old sheds was a bit odd... but Lou was getting used to it. After all – it had resulted in her glorious beach hut, which was fast becoming one of her favourite places in the whole world.

During their giggle-fest, Lou had told the girls about her fear that Sean might have a secret thing for model railways – given his involvement in the Paths and Sheds committee. About three bottles of wine into the evening, Hattie had dared Lou to demand to see his attic... just in case. This plan was promptly backed up by the other two, and so the four of them swayed and giggled their way over to Sand Piper Lane.

As soon as Sean had finished laughing at them all, he'd invited them in, handed them each a glass of water with orders to "drink up", and then dutifully fetched the loft ladder down so that Lou could check the evidence for herself. It had taken quite a bit of effort to get up those steps, but with Sean's hand steadying her backside, Lou had finally been able to see for herself. She'd almost been disappointed when all she'd found was a couple of cardboard boxes that were empty barring some dead spiders.

It was so wonderful being with a man who could take being teased and knew how to handle a group of giggling idiots when they turned up unannounced on his doorstep. He didn't go quiet – or sulk for days. Not like Brendan would have. But Lou was done with comparing Sean to Brendan – because there simply was no comparison. She was now with a man who made her laugh, who had a sense of humour, who...

...who was busy pulling on her ridiculous swimming cap covered in bright plastic flowers. Lou watched him with her mouth open, half covering her eyes at the sight.

With a *whoop* and a ridiculous jig, Sean started to

run towards the sea, only to be greeted by a sopping-wet Stanley who was barking happily at the appearance of his favourite swimming companion.

Lou scanned the beach, taking in the beaming gardeners and the giggling Dippers – all laughing and pointing at Sean's ridiculous antics. Oh, good grief… maybe this was the reason he usually swam on his own!

Lou shook her head and laughed out loud as she stared at the man who seemed to steal another chunk of her heart every single day she was with him.

Without her swimming cap, Lou knew that her hair would be a total mess later – but she couldn't care less. She had a beach hut in the garden where the sunshine streamed in through the window above. Later, the pair of them could curl up on the little sofa in front of the wood burner and get warm and cosy again.

But first… there were waves to be conquered, and salty seaside kisses to be stolen with the man she was falling in love with.

Lou dropped her towel and pelted down the beach to join the others in the sea.

THE END

Head back to Seabury for the start of Lizzie's story in
A Quiet Life in Seabury

ALSO BY BETH RAIN

Seabury Series:

Welcome to Seabury (Seabury Book 1)

Trouble in Seabury (Seabury Book 2)

Christmas in Seabury (Seabury Book 3)

Sandwiches in Seabury (Seabury Book 4)

Secrets in Seabury (Seabury Book 5)

Surprises in Seabury (Seabury Book 6)

Dreams and Ice Creams in Seabury (Seabury Book 7)

Mistakes and Heartbreaks in Seabury (Seabury Book 8)

Laughter and Happy Ever After in Seabury (Seabury Book 9)

A Quiet Life in Seabury (Seabury Book 10)

In A Spin in Seabury (Seabury Book 11)

Living The Dream in Seabury (Seabury Book 12)

A Big Day in Seabury (Seabury Book 13)

Something Borrowed in Seabury (Seabury Book 14)

A Match Made in Seabury (Seabury Book 15)

Seabury Series Collections:

Kate's Story: Books 1 - 3

Hattie's Story: Books 4 - 6

Standalones: Books 7 - 9

Lizzie's Story: Books 10 - 12

Upper Bamton Series:

Upper Bamton: The Complete Series Collection: Books 1 - 4

Individual titles:

A New Arrival in Upper Bamton (Upper Bamton Book 1)

Rainy Days in Upper Bamton (Upper Bamton Book 2)

Hidden Treasures in Upper Bamton (Upper Bamton Book 3)

Time Flies By in Upper Bamton (Upper Bamton Book 4)

Standalone Books:

How to be Angry at Christmas

Crumbleton Series:

Coming Home to Crumbleton (Crumbleton Book 1)

Flowers Go Flying in Crumbleton (Crumbleton Book 2)

Match Point in Crumbleton (Crumbleton Book 3)

A Very Crumbleton Christmas (Crumbleton Book 4)

Little Bamton Series:

Little Bamton: The Complete Series Collection: Books 1 - 5

Individual titles:

Christmas Lights and Snowball Fights (Little Bamton Book 1)

Spring Flowers and April Showers (Little Bamton Book 2)

Summer Nights and Pillow Fights (Little Bamton Book 3)

Autumn Cuddles and Muddy Puddles (Little Bamton Book 4)

Christmas Flings and Wedding Rings (Little Bamton Book 5)

Crumcarey Island Series:

Crumcarey Island Series Collection: Books 1 - 5

Individual titles:

Christmas on Crumcarey (Crumcarey Island Book 1)

All Change on Crumcarey (Crumcarey Island Book 2)

Making Waves on Crumcarey (Crumcarey Island Book 3)

Fool's Gold on Crumcarey (Crumcarey Island Book 4)

A Fresh Start on Crumcarey (Crumcarey Island Book 5)

WRITING AS BEA FOX

What's a Girl To Do? The Complete Series

Individual titles:

The Holiday: What's a Girl To Do? (Book 1)

The Wedding: What's a Girl To Do? (Book 2)

The Lookalike: What's a Girl To Do? (Book 3)

The Reunion: What's a Girl To Do? (Book 4)

At Christmas: What's a Girl To Do? (Book 5)

ABOUT THE AUTHOR

Beth Rain has always wanted to be a writer and has been penning adventures for characters ever since she learned to stare into the middle-distance and daydream.

She recently moved to a windswept, Scottish island, and it is a dream come true to spend her days hanging out with Bob – her trusty laptop – scoffing crisps and chocolate while dreaming up swoony love stories for all her imaginary friends.

Beth's writing will always deliver on the happy-ever-afters, so if you need cosy… you're in safe hands!

Visit www.bethrain.com for all the bookish goodness and keep up with all Beth's news by joining her newsletter!

        facebook.com/BethRainBooks
        twitter.com/bethrainauthor
        instagram.com/bethrainauthor

Printed in Dunstable, United Kingdom